THE BOOK OF WHY

THE BOOK OF WHY

J. BRADLEY MINNICK

This is a work of fiction. The characters and circumstances herein are products of the author's imagination and any resemblance to real places or people are merely a coincidence.

Copyright © 2026 by J. Bradley Minnick.

All rights reserved. No part of this publication may be reproduced without permission, except for brief quotations in reviews.

ISBNs: 978-1-971238-12-8 (paperback); 978-1-971238-13-5 (ebook)

Library of Congress Control Number: 2026935623

First Printing: 2026

Printed in the United States of America

Published by Silent Clamor Press, Los Angeles CA

"A Man's Reach Should Exceed His Grasp." First published in *Cleaver*, 2023.
Copyright © 2023 by J. Bradley Minnick

"The World Had Come For Us." First published in *East of the Web*, 2024.
Copyright © 2024 by J. Bradley Minnick

"The Day the End of the World Was at Hand." First published in *Literally Stories*, 2025.
Copyright © 2025 by J. Bradley Minnick

PRAISE FOR J. BRADLEY MINNICK

There is an air of mystery in everything J. Bradley Minnick writes. His prose and his characters—and even the neighborhoods and towns his characters inhabit—are in ceaseless search of the human soul. With a smiling, gentle sadness they offer abundant evidence of both its existence and its ungraspable nature. "The Pleasures of Sudden Wonder" is a glowing example of what makes Minnick such a special writer; like the houses that line its streets, this story will speak to you.

—Trent Lee Stewart author of
The Mysterious Benedict Society

J. Bradley Minnick's short stories are invariably infused with a lively combination of poignant humor and quirky wit. "Swimming for Fossils" is no exception. As its title hints, the story verges on the surreal while inviting us on a journey of introspective self-discovery — a journey told with characteristic verve in Minnick's unique style and poetic voice.

—Frank Thurmond, author of *Lottie Deno: A Novel of the Civil War and the American Southwest*

The first thing that one might notice about J. Bradley Minnick's finely crafted story, "The Day the End of the World Was at Hand," is the apocalyptic message in the title, a message that resonates on multiple levels throughout the story, especially as manifest in the loss of childhood innocence, the loss of idealized courage (as represented by the family car, the Plymouth Valiant), and the heartfelt loss of connections to the past. In a style and tone reminiscent of Harper Lee, Minnick creates a story that seamlessly weaves past and present, hope and fear, and love and loss. It is a story that demands a close and careful reading (and re-readings!), so that the promise and payoff of the anagogical nature of its reality, as Flannery O'Connor suggests, may be fully and wonderfully realized.

—Keith Polette, author of
Soundings and *Isabel & The Hungry Coyote*

"The World Has Come For Us" is a hauntingly evocative coming-of-age story that pedals straight from the sun-drenched thrill of summer into the wrenching collision of innocence with the larger world beyond. With precision, J. Bradley Minnick draws us into the idiosyncratic universe of a young boy, where toy cars, pedal-powered adventures, and unbreakable bonds give way to the realities of scorching heat, silence, and fear. At once tender and unsettling, this story captures the fragile heartbeat of childhood and the way a single day can exist at the nexus between innocence and growing up.

—Ryan Scribner Editor of
The GroundUp literary magazine

For Mom

"What is fate but density of childhood"

—Rainer Maria Rilke

CONTENTS

Introduction	xv
1. A Man's Reach should Exceed his Grasp	1
2. The Everyday Street, Full of the Common Everyday Scene	17
3. The World Had Come For Us	29
4. The Book of Why	43
5. Swimming for Fossils	55
6. The Day the End of the World Was At Hand	71
7. The Pleasures of Sudden Wonder	83
Notes	105
Acknowledgments	107
Illustrator Biography	109
About the Author	111
Also by J. Bradley Minnick	113

INTRODUCTION

I've always been fascinated by cycle stories–some call them connected story collections, but I've never gone in for that term. My love for cycle stories began with Sherwood Anderson's 1919 book *Winesburg, Ohio* (full title: *Winesburg, Ohio: A Group of Tales of Ohio Small-Town Life*)–22 stories set in a single place. Anderson's characters–he thinks of them as "grotesques"–move in and out of the stories, often appearing in one and then reappearing in another. Sadly, however, except for George Willard, the protagonist, a boy who wants to be a writer–most of the characters are trapped and can't seem to find a way out of the town. Even George has second thoughts, after having a fight with his foe, Elmer Cowley, before leaving Winesburg, Ohio by train to begin his life.

My love for *Winesburg, Ohio* is also personal. My grandfather knew "Old Man Anderson," who, after Anderson's successes and failures, had set up shop as a writer and editor and owner of two Marion, Virginia newspapers–one town over from where my grandfather lived.

Anderson's gravestone, a large concrete sculpture, is in the Round Hill Cemetery in Marion. I know this first hand as I had my mother go with me as I trekked across the weedy cemetery in search of it. When we finally came upon what looked like a witch's hat that seemed to rise up out of the earth and point toward the sky, I was left with an indelible imprint of that moment and a terrible case of poison ivy.

What I've come to see as essential elements of cycle story books like *Winsburg, Ohio,* John Steinbeck's *Pastures of Heaven* and *Tortilla Flat,* Louis Nordan's *Music of the Swamp,* and John Updike's *Olinger Stories* is a firm and deep-seated sense of place (the real places that the above authors modeled into fiction were Clyde, Ohio; Salinas and San Francisco, California; Itta Bena, Mississippi; and Shillington, Pennsylvania). And, yet, this sense of place and the antiquated objects that inhabit them are emblematic of a particular period of time, sadly, that is not quite there anymore.

The *Book of Why's* protagonist, Jayson Why morphed from a character I created in college I named Y–a young boy who found himself in impossible and sometimes mundane predicaments, which he turned Walter Mitty-like into fantastical situations. I still have those old Y stories in a drawer in my mother's house, and even reworked the best of one of them into this cycle story book.

INTRODUCTION

Writing and rewriting these cycle stories about a fictionalized 60s American suburban neighborhood taught me to pay attention to that moment in time, to the fictional Winsome Street, to Al Kaline (the big tree, in protagonist Jayson Why's front lawn), to Dizzy Gillespie (the light pole that Jayson whirls around); to the strange houses in Netherlands, and, to the big white house on the hill. The world Jayson Why lives in is insulated from the horrors of the Vietnam War, at least for a little while. Yet, the outside world creeps in–it can't help itself, and it reaches out its hands and takes a large portion of everyone's appetite.

Our real house in Detroit, the setting for many of these cycle stories, was as small inside as our front yard was big. There was the garage, the living room, which featured the television front and center, the kitchen, and the three small back bedrooms. My parents weren't much for decorations and let the past stand. The furniture in our living room was the same as it had been in our Philadelphia house. If I wished hard enough, I could convince myself that we had never left the city of Brotherly Love.

The really cool feature of our house for me, however, was our basement. In the basement, my mother created a perfect facsimile of a "family room." All of the wicker furniture (that looked like tree limbs)—a rocking chair and a piano from our Philadelphia house. There was also a fireplace.

I was a sensitive child, and my mother learned early that she had to frame her words carefully. Mom bought me an electric pen, and when it was turned on, I felt I was able to create a language that only I believed I could read. I loved our basement, and I spent as much time as I could down there with my imaginary purple friend named V in a room off to the side, pretending to swing from the peppermint striped trapeze that was tied to the ceiling high above the washing machine.

I would find my way home from school and immediately go down the steps and sit in the dark. I do know that my mother didn't like to spend very much time down in the basement herself. I suppose she was running away from the past as much as I was trying to fall back into it.

In writing these stories, one of my hopes was to make the mundane fantastical. That's what we hope for in life right? And indeed Jayson Why finds himself in mundane, yet impossible positions that he must find his way out of: swimming lessons at the Y.M.C.A.; telling impossible lies; marching around in circles at a 4th of July picnic; and, playing in a deep hole on Winsome street trying to uncover the city's past. In one sense Jayson has put himself in no-win positions, and, in another, at least in his mind, these no-win positions have crept up on him. What if, then, he steadfastly refuses to grow up? Another impossible position. And, in *The Book of Why* change is not welcomed. Jayson Why wants to slow things down so much that he can handle the daily objects that present themselves–his bike, his toy car, his father's Super 8 movie camera. As he looks back, he wants to slow time and return to an analog world and a protected suburban life that no-longer exists; he wants to examine class distinctions and social interaction. These stories take place around the time of the Apollo space missions–a moment when America lost its innocence.

And there are truths in these stories: "A Man's Reach Should Exceed His Grasp" is the saying on my father's gravestone. The title story, "The Book of Why" reconsiders the popular television soap opera *Dark Shadows* (with vampire Barnabus Collins). The last story, "The Pleasures of Sudden Wonder" takes up Gaston Bachelard's *The Poetics of Space* as it discusses the importance of one's first house, of attics, of basements, and of miniatures. Note the details from the four prongs in the upper left hand corner of the front cover (indicating this is a journal–indeed The Book of Why) to the miniature book cover of Gaston Bachelard's *The Poetics of Space* in Erika's hands in final story "The Pleasures of Sudden Wonder." Bachelard, I think, would appreciate these "miniatures."

I'd be remiss if I didn't comment on the illustrations, created by the amazing artist L.K. Sukany. During our numerous discussions, we came to imagine these illustrations working together as a kind of old-time flip-book–a paper book that when flipped through quickly tells a larger story. In particular the drawings of Jason Why, whose hands are in the air like a Y (an homage to the original Y character) suggest a setting that remains the same, while the perspective changes– in front of Jason is an oncoming Plymouth Valiant, Kate Wheeler standing on the seat of her bike, and the big wide wonderful sky.

Time springs forth eternal and the world hears more than one word at a time—at least in retrospect. I hope my future self, as he reads these stories, enjoys spending time in that neighborhood, in the Netherlands, and on Winsome street. I hope that in some distant future, as I read these stories aloud, I say to myself, "That one was pretty good; that one worked."

A MAN'S REACH SHOULD EXCEED HIS GRASP

My mother arranged for us to walk to school together. I didn't want to go to school; and, I especially didn't want to walk anywhere with Kate Wheeler.

Kate Wheeler was my next-door neighbor. She was as persistent as she was pretty, as forthright as she was forceful. She had no shame, and I had so much.

She appeared at my front door on the first day of 1st grade and rang the bell. No one ever came to the front door or rang the bell. My mother opened the door and Kate said, "It's raining today, Mrs. Why. Does Jayson have his umbrella, or should I run home and get one for him?"

I felt remarkably self-conscious as I hid behind my mother. As her palm pushed me through the doorway, she handed me my paper lunch bag full of all those sandwiches I could never stomach.

Kate, who was my age, actually had the audacity to grab my hand like she was leading a little boy who couldn't possibly find his way without help. "Come with me, Jayson!" Kate said in a very patient voice, showing off to my mother, who, caught in the grip of my agony, returned a condescending smile.

I really wouldn't have minded so much if Kate hadn't seemed so perfect to me at that moment with her straight, white teeth, her two older sisters (both beautiful), her father's Corvette convertible parked on a paved driveway in front of her house, and her long backyard with the swimming pool.

And, I imagined what she must have thought of me with my father's black Plymouth Valiant with holes in the floorboards, with our gravel driveway with the small stones that hurt your feet, and with my baby sister, only six months old, who could hardly be considered human yet.

And above and beyond all of her worldly possessions, Kate Wheeler had learned, in a matter of weeks, to ride her purple two-wheeler with the shiny chrome handlebars and the perfect banana seat.

Every evening at exactly 6:30, she would flit past my two-wheeler, a red Western Auto Cosmic Flyer that had become, more or less, a permanent fixture leaning on its kickstand. Then, at precisely 6:35, she would zoom past my front door again, this time on the other side of the street, while big automobiles brushed past her creating unnatural breezes that kept Kate aloft on her perfect banana seat.

My father's motto, and sadly I must say it is not an original one, borrowed from Robert Browning, went like this: "Ah, but a man's reach should exceed his grasp, or what's a heaven for?"[1] Father reworked the line into, "One might reach and never get a firm grasp."

My father read Browning's poetry to me every night in place of fairy tales: Robert Browning's poetry raised my earthly existence, swooping me up in dizzy exhilaration, bypassing reality and climbing into my dreams.

My father pulled the box marked "This Side Up" out of the back of the Plymouth Valiant. It wasn't even my birthday, but he explained the bicycle was a birthday present in advance. Two hours later the assembled bike leaned on its kickstand in our garage, a bright, shiny victim of gravity.

"Let's ride it," Father said.

"That's okay," I said.

"Don't you like it?"

"Sure, I like it. I love it, but, I just want to look at it for a while."

"Here, let's wheel it outside on the cement and I'll give you a push."

I wasn't sure which word most prevented my willingness to reach out and grasp, cement or push.

"That's okay," I said.

"Come on," he said. "Let's give it a try."

I hated every minute of that first day Kate and I

walked to school, her cool hand clenched my sweaty one. We crossed the street and walked through a mysterious region I called the Netherlands where the sidewalk was dark and the tops of the trees blotted out the sun.

The houses in the Netherlands were much darker and seemed sad: sad houses that never smiled and cast oblong shadows on lawns too lush to walk on; stately affairs with drab trim, painted shutters and pillars. Houses in the Netherlands reminded me of disapproving adults who looked down from towering heights. As I passed each house, I made up names for each in my head: Mr. Honesty, Ms. Books, Mr. Bike, Ms. Western, Mr. Auto.

My father wheeled my two-wheeler out of our garage. "Hop on," he said.

"What do you mean?"

"Just get on," he said. "The rest will take care of itself."

"Like this?"

"Does it feel right?"

"I don't know," I said, straddling the heart-shaped seat.

"You're not supposed to," he said, "but, you will know when you know."

"I will?"

"Let's go!" he said.

School was a funny place filled with too much

concrete and too many colors. Kids were everywhere. Some were holding their mother's hands, others their legs, and the really shy ones, their behinds. Kate grabbed my hand tight and pulled me through the schoolyard. There was something about holding a mother's hand that didn't call attention to you. There was something about holding Kate Wheeler's hand that wasn't quite right.

"My father walked through this with me yesterday, so I know where we're going."

Kate had used Labor Day afternoon, no less, to walk around the school and find our 1st grade classroom with her father, who owned a Corvette convertible and for all I knew, the world.

Busses pulled up to painted curbs. It was the first time I had seen a school bus and I couldn't imagine the skill and know-how it must have taken to ride one. The big yellow machines were filled with kids from great distances away.

Why shouldn't Kate be in charge? She had learned to ride her bicycle the right-proper-way, one step at a time, while I had been thrown into the thick of grasping air, applying pushes to principles that exceeded my grasp.

"You've got to push the pedals to make them work!" my father said.

"How do I do that?"

"Push down on them."

"I can't!"

"Don't say you can't, say you won't!"

"I can't, and when I push backwards, the pedals won't work either."

"No, if you push on the pedals backwards, you activate the brake."

"Won't I go backwards?"

"No, you'll stop. Your problem is that your pedals are too far back and you can't get proper leverage."

"Don't say can't, say won't," I said.

"Push the pedals half-way round to go forward."

"Show me!"

I am told by my mother that Kate and I walked on separate sides of the street on the way home from school that first day. Our hand-holding days, it seemed, were over. Why? I'm not sure. My guess is that Kate had been too bossy.

"You won't know when I let you go, but whatever you do, don't stop pedaling," my father said.

I could feel him running beside me. The wheel of my Cosmic Flyer hummed against the unevenness of an overgrown sidewalk.

"Don't let me go," I wailed into the air.

"I've got you!" he said. "Keep pedaling!"

"This is fun!" I said.

He said I wouldn't know when he let me go, but somehow I knew, and I stopped pedaling.

"Why don't you carry a lunch bag to school?" I said to Kate the second day while we walked to school.

"Because I have money and buy my lunch at school along with a container of cold milk." From the depths of a little purse made of colored beads and zippers, Kate extracted a dollar.

"I'm allergic to milk," I said.

"You're supposed to fall down the first time," my father said.

"Why didn't you tell me?"

"Are you okay?"

"It's like I'm drowning in a sidewalk sea."

"Let's try again."

"I think I scratched the bike."

When I saw the dollar in Kate's hand, that's when I got the idea to sell lies.

"I know something you don't," I said.

"What?"

"I just do," I said and left it at that for a while.

"Hop on again," Father said.

"I'm afraid I will fall again," I said.

"Come on, give it a try," he said.

"It's full of falling," I said.

"Okay," he said, finally. "Let's go polish this scratch."

At that very instant, Kate Wheeler rode by on her bicycle and waved to me with one hand while I stood defeated on the pavement. Two little wheels trailed on each side of Kate's back wheel; those little wheels kept her going; they kept her up; they kept that interminable smile on her face.

"Look!" I said, "Kate Wheeler has those extra wheels!"

"They're called training wheels, Jayson," my father said, "and you don't need them."

"I don't?"

So, I didn't have training wheels either, just like we didn't have a Corvette convertible for our driveway or a pool in our backyard.

"I know what we're getting for Christmas," I said to Kate. I was about to sell my first lie.

"I just love Christmas!" Kate said.

"Our parents are going in together and buying the present for both of us, a special Christmas treat."

"Tell me!" Kate said. "I love treats!"

"For a dollar," I said.

"Okay," she said and reached into her purse and forked-over the dollar.

"A tent for us to play in."

Kate looked skeptical. "A big one," I spread my hands wide, "that we can set up in the front yard and play in."

"How do you know?"

"I overheard my mom talking to your mom on the phone."

"Really? Wow!"

"And we can play all kinds of games."

"Like house," Kate said.

"I guess."

"And you can be the mommy and I'll be the daddy."

"I want to be the daddy," I said.

"Oh, I've always wanted a house," she said. "With dishes and plates and you'll go off to work."

"Wait a minute," I said.

I am going to Hell for sure, I thought that night.

"I know something you don't know," I said on our walk to school.

"What?"

"For a dollar."

Kate reached into her beaded purse and gingerly handed me a dollar.

"My father's going to buy a new car," I said.

"What kind?" Kate said.

"You've seen it," I said. "It's the Bloom's rag top Cadillac."

"Then, it's not new," Kate said.

"No," I said. "It's not new."

"And that wasn't worth a dollar, Jayson. Give it back!"

There was no selling the truth.

Kate continued to zip by my front door on her bike every evening at exactly 6:30. She had also taken to riding in the street. She had replaced the large training wheels with a set of smaller ones that only touched down occasionally.

My Cosmic Flyer leaned against its kickstand in the middle of our gravel drive for the better part of a month. My father never pushed me to ride it again.

"I know what we're starting next week," I said.

"What?"

"For a dollar."

She had it ready before I even asked, pressing it into my palm.

"Ballet lessons!"

"Really?"

"Yes, you and me and some other kids are going to start taking them next week."

"Really?"

"Yes, it's supposed to help me with coordination, for sports, you know?"

"Coordination?"

"Yes, and Janice Pastiche is going to give them."

"The cheerleader?"

"Yes."

"With the red car and the long hair and the beads around her neck?"

"Yes."

"I can't believe it."

"You won't believe it!" I said.

"I don't believe it," Kate said. "Give me back the dollar."

"It's the honest to God's truth," I lied.

"Now I can get pink ballet slippers and fly through the air. You can throw me."

"What?"

"And I can do pirouettes in toe shoes like I'm gliding on clouds. You can catch me."

"Wait a minute."

"I can't wait! And, I need that dollar to buy the slippers."

"Don't let your mom know you know. It's supposed to be a surprise. And maybe afterward we can swim in your pool, like a party?"

"I don't know," she said. "My dad can't get the chlorine right."

Like clockwork, Kate cruised by my front door that night. Her legs worked the pedals, and her dress swirled behind her caught by the breeze. I blinked my eyes when she raced past, her wheels jumping a curb and spinning onto the street.

A big car breezed by her. A family rode in the front seat oblivious to the outside world, speaking in hands. An old lady sat in the back seat watching Kate. I made up a name for her out of my head; I called her Mrs. Wings. Mrs. Wings watched Kate from the back window and clapped her hands. Mrs. Wings clapped because Kate was riding her purple bicycle with the shiny handlebars and the perfect banana seat without any training wheels at all.

I had to find a way to stop the purple nightmares. In

them, I would push my bike to the top of the winding hill in the Netherlands. I would sit proudly on the seat and gaze down upon the steep sidewalk lined with the sad houses. I wouldn't want to, but halfway down I would stop pedaling, and fall out of the sky. Blood would pour forth from my skin. It would be purple.

The day that I made up my mind that I was going to learn to ride my Western Auto Cosmic Flyer bicycle was the same day that I sold the big lie.

"I can do something you can't!" I said.

"What?" Kate Wheeler said.

"I'll teach you how if you want."

Kate dropped my hand she still held once in a while and surrendered a dollar.

"This better be good."

"It's the best one yet."

"Well, what?" she said.

"I promise you won't regret it."

"I'll just bet!"

"Completely and utterly true."

"Just say it."

"As God is my witness," I said.

"And start praying that I care enough not to smack you."

"And mother's back on a sidewalk crack."

"I'm hungry all of the time now."

"I can fly," I said.

"Oh, you cannot, Jayson! Give me back my dollar!" she said.

I held her dollar out to the air.

"Just like Superman."

"The milk used to be so cold."

"Just like a bird," I said.

"And the lunch raviolis were the best."

"I promise to show you how after school, Kate."

"No fair! Give me back my lunch money."

"It might take a little practice, but once I show you, it'll be all you'll need!"

"If this doesn't work, Jayson. I'm telling my father."

"It'll work."

"And, he'll tell your father."

"I know."

"And, you'll never be able to sit down again."

"I know."

"Much less fly."

"I know."

"Or, tell lies."

That afternoon, Kate and I were sitting aslant on our bikes on top of the hill in the Netherlands. It was just like in the purple nightmares, but I was really here this time.

The sad houses were below us, and looking at us: Mr. Honesty, Ms. Books, Ms. Western, Mr. Auto, Mr. Bike. I stared at the sun until I couldn't see anything but the black outlines of the tall trees.

"Teach me how to fly, Jayson."

"Okay, but it's sort of complicated."

"Yeah, right, just like I thought," Kate said, "Give me back my dollar."

"First, you have to stand up on the seat."

"You're crazy."

"No, Kate, that's the first thing. I swear to God on my mother's headstone. Like this."

I pushed the pedal around so I would get the proper leverage, stood on the back pedal and balanced one foot on my heart-shaped seat.

"Now, you try."

"This is dangerous, Jayson."

"Come on, don't be a fraidy cat."

"Don't call me a fraidy cat."

"Then, try."

Kate kicked down the kickstand, leveled her pedals with her hand, and used the back pedal to step up with one foot on the perfect banana seat.

"Now what?"

"Now we have to say the magic words."

"What words?"

"The special magic ones."

"I can't stand up here forever."

"I will say them first and then you repeat after me."

"Hurry."

"Roses are red."

"Roses are red."

"Budweiser's my brew."

"What does that mean?"

"My dad drinks Budweiser. Just say it."

"Budweiser's my brew."

"It won't work unless you mean it."

"BREW!"

"Now for the tricky part."

"Now for the tricky part."

"No, I'm just telling you that the next part is tricky. Now go, first."

"Go first?"

"Yes, go first."

"I don't want to."

"Sure you do. And it's guaranteed to work."

"Guaranteed?"

"Right. Now repeat after me."

"Okay."

"I'll ride down the road."

"I'll ride down the road."

"And fly after you."

"And fly after you."

"After you."

"Me?"

"Yes, I'll be right behind you."

"Promise?"

"I swear on my father's head."

Then, without hesitation, Kate started her journey down into the Netherlands, standing with one perfect foot on top of her perfect banana-shaped seat, hovering over the darkened sidewalk, breezing through the tall trees, and flying past each sad house as a real person took its place: Ms. Books, Mr. Honesty, Ms. Western, Mr. Auto, Mr. Bike and even Mrs. Wings stood there on otherwise barren lawns smiling and clapping at Kate

Wheeler's perfect flying form. When she safely reached the bottom of the hill, she sat down with a plop, popped a wheelie, started her slow climb back up the hill toward me, and said as perfectly as you please, "You didn't follow, Jayson. You promised you'd be right behind. Are you a fraidy cat? You owe me a dollar. I'll watch you fly this time. Ride down the road. And I'll fly after you."

THE EVERYDAY STREET, FULL OF THE COMMON EVERYDAY SCENE

So, there we all were perambulating without purpose in a celebration of sameness—the adults avoiding bumping into the vinyl-covered card tables and straight-backed dining room chairs, we kids, in perpetual motion, didn't want to be caught dead standing in one place too long—often running smack into adults, who would make us to say our "sorry's," pick us up before we began to cry, and, like wind-up toys, send us back out into our confined worlds: self-selected by grade, age, class, even words, which were, at the same time, sloppy and precise.

So, you might imagine our surprise when the Medleys with Glen in tow showed up. My mother wrote down in her ledger, "And they never showed up to anything." Except for Glen, I don't think anyone *but* my mother knew their first names, and we certainly didn't know what they did for a living.

The balance of our summers was never really hot, but 4th of July's for some reason were always scorchers: an incontrovertible truth (and it wasn't as if we could bring our summer fans outside or that they would do any good if we did). With most of the neighbors approaching what they officially knew to be their end of their youths—they substituted cheerleading practice and running around in cleats for the taste of cranking out summer ice cream from their old-fashioned ice cream makers and the boredom of annual 4th of July Block Parties on our front lawn, which, through some stroke of luck, was the most expansive on Winsome Street.

Glen Medley must have been a surprise package. My mother wrote in her ledger that she imagined Irene Medley, 46, couldn't believe, even after he'd been born, that Glen had happened to her. And, in school we ignored Glen. I'm not sure why. He wasn't particularly odd, nor was he what we would have called weird. He kept to himself, fiddled with mechanical things: built a scooter, took apart a television set, used a can opener's motor to power a wooden skateboard, and played in the school band. He wore suits to class with clip-on ties and plaid shirts and different colored socks; the suit sleeves hung over his hands, which were always in motion.

Glen Medley was like a perturbed adult dropped in

our midst, complaining about Richard Nixon and at 13 espousing rationality, protesting by quoting Kant. There was a rumor he'd been to see *Easy Rider* before his birthday. There was another rumor he ironed his own clothes and bought all the groceries for the family. He showed up to school on his scooter and chained it to the bike rack with a lock he'd made himself, whose horizontal numbers read 0000. During lunch recess, we tried to crack the code. Whenever Glen Medley saw us fiddling with his lock, he'd smile, and leave us to our failures. He was rational and sane and because he was, we thought him mad and insane. We waited for him to do something notorious; instead he won the school competition for long-division and gave his trophy away to the librarian, who displayed it behind the front counter for all to see if ever, and this was rare, we were forced to checkout some book or another. His rationality let out a kind of honest rage in us, but, because of the heat, we were already red-faced and profoundly unhappy with ourselves and how we looked in each other's eyes. And, yet when we saw Glen, we looked *into* each other's eyes. We were bad actors but good-acting neighbors and surprised ourselves with hearty welcomes and good cheer.

Believe me, I know this sounds strange, but my mother carried around a big old ledger book that her father—a nervous accountant—had used for figures most of his life. For my mother, this ledger documented the collective cares of everyone on Winsome Street, or at least everyone who attended those awful summer 4th of July Block Parties. And like a good Lois Lane, there she would be, holding a pen as if she were holding a microphone. Much of her reportage would later find its way into *The Winsome Street Newsletter* that she typed out on an old Underwood (my father's) and distributed door-to-door.

So, when the Medleys showed up at our Block Party, pretending a bathroom break, I took up my mother's footsteps and bolted into our squat red brick house and unearthed the Super 8 movie camera. Earlier in the summer, my father had taken me with him downtown and had seen the Super 8 in the window of Truly's Television & Repair Shop. He had told me, although I imagined that he was telling as much to himself, that he had to have it—to possess it. And to justify having it, he'd gift it to my mother, who, he said, could capture the events and moments that represented in reality the day-to-day of a life that seemed to go nowhere, even in my mother's ledgers, and that represented—he said to himself—"No real beginning or ending but a perpetual middle trying to find its mark."

There was hope in my father's eyes when he handed Mr. Truly all of the bills he had in his fat homemade wallet; and Mr. Truly handed over the box, implored my father to read the directions, said that it was the first

Super 8 he'd sold and that my father was certainly the first person on Winsome Street to own one.

Like he did whenever he bought a new pair of shoes, my father let the camera sit in the box for a good long while as he got used to the idea of the money he'd spent money on it. Finally, he gave it to my mother for her June birthday, taking in her odd expression as he eyed her journals stacked on top of one another in the corner of the dining room. "This," he said, "is for capturing reality."

We hadn't expected the Medleys to show up to our July 4th Block Party, but once they did, it felt as if they'd always been there in our midst—as if the Super 8 had always been rolling, as if we kids had forever been spontaneously marching in an ordered circle around the yard—holding flags, waving sparklers, knees high—marching, marching, marching around the periphery of the chairs and vinyl-covered tables. And usually out of the frame were glimpses of tired adults, who all looked uptight and were bent on staying right where they were in that this was being put down for posterity—with the clicking sound of a projector already imagined as a kind of backdrop for future screenings of past events. The constant clicking substituting for voices and one could almost hear the chattering from inside my mother's journals come to life through the projector's gears.

As if displaying the desire to metaphorically sit at

the kid's tables, the Medleys joined the line of marching children, and, except for Glen, began marching too. This was when I must have handed the camera off to my mother—who began filming—because there I am, marching, too; my big head aware and unaware of what I am doing, fixated on the tiny flag I am waving, eyeing with envy cousin Jimmy Why, Jr., who is holding a sparkler in one hand and his ever-present trick-or-treat suitcase, which trails behind him.

It's a strange feeling to see your living and breathing self that you don't remember; but there I am, sure as shooting, with I don't know what on my mind. It's also strange for neighbors who you never really knew to adapt so easily into a children's marching line, and the Medleys marched like shadows dissipating with light. Were they doing this for their own amusement? Were they poking fun at the rituals that had become us? Had they wanted to show us what, in their eyes and while previously looking at us through their sad windows, we had all become? Or, were they innocents, joining us without a thought, marching with us around the tables and chairs, holding little flags, wary of the sparklers?

In the film, the Medleys for all practical purposes are the only adults present. There was Hebert Medley with a crew-cut smile and 5 o'clock shadow. There was Irene Medley, who looked like a beneficent Sunday school teacher marching around the periphery of the tables and once in a while straightening a displaced chair or picking up a fallen napkin. And there was Glen Medley, who stood off to the side, alone, refusing to join our continuous circle, which suggested no beginning and no end. And, as the circularity of life played out in front of him, it was clear that he was truly miserable, that he was the only one present with enough presence to be himself. And, I wonder as I watch this film some thirty years later, why some part of us couldn't be like Glen. And I believe were he to inherit the world, he would have known what to do with it.

We were play acting after all; yet, at a block party's notice, our fealty to the best laid plans held us in check: our manners followed us through the remainder of the week; but, our disappointment in ourselves never really faded like we'd hoped. Maybe these bad actors were the worst parts of ourselves who craved attention or to be let out of doors for at least one hot summer day? We couldn't escape ourselves. I'm not so sure we really wanted to. We could not keep consistency through blatant inconsistency, so we carried on as we sifted through the ensuing decades waiting to uncover something we had missed seeing. Instead, it was easier to dust off our old skins and fit inside our well-worn selves—to settle for less, to acknowledge we were missing something of a cultural center. Perhaps there was something out of the frame we weren't meant to see. Perhaps, someone down the line was looking at us —trying to figure us out—considering what we would do next.

And then occurs the single oddest thing right there and right then. Glen walks into the center of the circle while all march around him; he smiles falsely and begins flipping over the chairs, one-by-one. Soon each lay like a misplaced doorstop on the lawn. Then, he bends down, getting underneath each table and explodes upward: the card tables fly off in all directions.

Out of some compulsion to keep order, the marching line quickens, knees rise higher, and it never occurs to my mother to shut the camera down.

Even now, part of me wants to join my younger self marching and another part wants to join Glen under the tables and upturn them.

Oddly, then, the scene shifts and my mother begins using the close-up feature, filming the surrounding houses that look as if they are watching us—their windows, tired eyes, their doors, closed mouths—their insides open without blinds drawn.

First, she focuses on our house with its green shutters and its red bricks, its rows of window boxes, its path that swells with uneven blocks of concrete running toward our front door. Then she focuses on the Medley's house across the street so like and unlike our own, and, it looks to be singing—its front door wide open, inviting any of us inside for iced tea, for ice cream, for a sugar cookie, showing its insides for all of us to see.

And, in her ledger book, through some strange obligation, my mother memorialized the afternoon ("Watched Cousin Jimmy Jr.'s suitcase spark on fire," "The workman dug up Winsome Street again and left a hole as deep as an elevator shaft," "The light pole's afternoon flickers gives me migraines") and provided descriptions ("The dandelions are as yellow as the monarchs," "The tables' legs are sinking into the ground like post-holes," "Winsome's Meats supplied the hamburger patties, yet I don't know if we'll patronize them next year," "The large tree has an old green scar that might be mold,"); and even noted silence ("Father smiles over the grill," "The tables are shimmering in the heat," "The bumble bees' hum mixes with the overhead wires"). My mother noted everything—the self-appointed official ethnographer of our neighborhood culture. My mother noted everything except this.

*The title of this story was taken from Wright Morris

THE WORLD HAD COME FOR US

My friend Manny Tankin had a toy truck; a perfect replica in miniature, a black nemesis with a flatbed, a working tailgate, and a cab one could sit in and pedal down the street. He named it Stegosaurus—"Stego" for short. I was less adventurous. I had a toy car, a little red job with finely crafted metal all around, steel headlights, and, of course, a set of pedals. I named it Ptarmigan—"Tar" for short.

That summer, Manny and I would meet on the sidewalk at dawn, shake hands in my gravel drive, return to Stego and Tar, hop in, and pedal with blinding fury until we smashed into each other. Then, we would sit in the cars—still as could be—faces frozen in mock agony, and imagine we were dead. Our brief affair with head-on collisions ended one morning in late August when Manny, in a panic after desperately searching for me, forgot to park Stego in the garage and left it behind the back wheels of his father's Chevrolet. Tears running down his cheeks, he told my mother that Stego had tried to prevent its own demise by emitting a loud, low, awful scream, but alas, he cried, "It was too late."

I was eleven and had, much to my father's dismay, taken to calling him, "Mr. Why" because I supposed I could ask him anything about just about anything, and I was confident he would supply the right-proper answer. Mr. Why owned a perfectly awful car—a Plymouth Valiant I named The Hipposaurus—"Hippo" for short, and I hated just about everything about it: it was black my least favorite color; its windows stuck in winter and in summer; its doors were heavy; its gear shift shot out of the floor and made great groaning sounds; its horn stuck fast and blared until you pounded on it to put it out; its grill looked like two lopsided front teeth in a cartoon; and, its broken odometer had stopped somewhere around 200,000 miles.

If you could have seen Hippo, you would have thought it was positively awful, too, but inexplicably Mr. Why loved it, adored it, refused to let it go; so, Mrs. Why and I just had to put up with it. Impossibly old, cranky, and loud, Hippo had acquired holes in its rotting floorboards so that one could watch the road as it passed underneath. Mrs. Why and I made-up a game of naming the roadways: Bumpy, Pothole, Slick, Trolley.

It was a perfectly lovely late August morning. Adventure was popping around my head like eggs on a griddle. I sneaked out of the house particularly early and stood in the middle of the sidewalk waiting for Manny and appraising the sunrise, the cool air, the fresh dew. A huge oak tree overarched our gravel drive I named Al Kaline—after the baseball player—its branches touching Heaven. Marigolds in yellow and orange lined the front of our house. Mr. Why had recently replanted them after in a monumental moment of exasperation I had taken my big plastic golf club to their innocent heads, whacking the fluttering colors everywhere. He hadn't been at all happy and kept repeating, "Why, Jayson, why?"

As I stood in the middle of the sidewalk that summer morning, all the possibilities of the day ended before they began: I imagined the scene that evening as kids of all shapes ran about in the middle of our front yard trying to play football. I imagined 5:00 p.m. sharp when Mr. Why would swing Hippo into the gravel drive, get out, take off his jacket, studiously lay it on the hood, slam the door with a kick, and hold up his hands for the football.

Al Kaline would cover us with shade as we would break from the huddle, line up in a row, and then run to the far reaches of the lawn trying to catch up with the spiral that hung in the air. We'd find ourselves in a great clump waiting for it to choose one of us. Then, the football would crash down like a missile, knocking the wind out of the chosen one, and after to the ground, where we'd all leap on top in a giant scrum and try to pry fingers from the ball so that we alone might emerge victorious. Then, usually in defeat, we'd all trot back to the huddle to repeat the glorious struggle, while the winner would get to throw ball on back to Mr. Why and then, in the huddle call, the next play.

That morning after looking to Al Kaline for answers to what lay beyond its tentacled shadows, I silently crept onto the gravel drive, careful not to damage my pristine tennis shoes on its sharp stones, pried open Hippo's heavy door, crunched way down in its backseat, and waited for my father. From inside Hippo, I heard Mr. Why open our front door and kiss Mrs. Why goodbye. His tired brogues made loud crunching noises in the gravel; he yanked open the car door, settled in the front seat with a grunt, switched on the radio to Morning Mystery Theatre, and backed out of the drive. Hippo hesitated in the street somewhere between reverse and first gear, groaned, and then surged ahead.

At that moment I realized I had made a stupendous mistake—more of a mistake even than when I destroyed the flowers. Believe you me, I *wanted* to tell Mr. Why I was hiding in the backseat. I wanted to tap him on the top of the head and say, "Hi ya, Mr. Why, funny meeting you here," so I could take my verbal lumps, endure his exasperated sigh, and rejoin the familiarity of the day. I couldn't. I shouldn't. I didn't say a word. Instead, I just sat there all crunched up in the backseat as Hippo left the trees, the replanted flowers, and our gravel drive behind.

We turned off Bumpy onto Patchy and then onto Hum. Out the rear window, smoke curled into the sky, cast off from factories that worked overtime.

By now Manny Tankin was certainly up, sitting at his kitchen table wolfing down his breakfast, preparing to open the heavy garage doors so that he could jump curbs, meet me in the front of my house, shake hands, and ride Stego like a tornado into Tar.

I imagined Mrs. Why sitting in the breakfast nook, drinking her morning coffee, unaware I was gone.

Manny would be revving his truck engine on our front walk, his feet nervous on the pedals, waiting impatiently for Tar to appear.

Mrs. Why would set down her coffee cup with a clink. The house was too quiet. Something just wasn't right.

We drove by the great steel plants that manufactured the sides, fronts, backs and bumpers of cars. The plants had not yet been torn down. Front gates had not yet disintegrated, and broken smokestacks had not yet loomed up like fragmented hulls on great ships run ashore in economic storms. Even from inside the car, I breathed in the fiery glow of furnaces, the smell of coke as The Hippo breezed past gates and fiery smokestacks.

Manny, tired of waiting for me, hopped out of Stego and hesitantly walked up the lonely stretch toward our front door. He made his way past the antique lamp post, stopped momentarily to look at the freshly planted flowers, smiled up at Al Kaline, pushed our doorbell and waited for the ring.

Standing in the open doorway, Mrs. Why with coffee cup in one hand and the doorknob in the other, considered Manny Tankin's sad, awful frown and looked out beyond him toward Stego sitting askance on the lonely sidewalk.

Factories turned into long buildings and then into immense parking lots filled with trucks and cars. Cars, in every possible parking space. The world was made up of cars.

Mr. Why maneuvered into a parking space, grabbed his briefcase in one hand and opened Hippo's car door with the other. The sun's rays hit the side of his face an instant before he closed the heavy car door and walked across the parking lot.

Mrs. Why ran into my bedroom, checking in every conceivable place. She even looked under my bed to see if I was hiding there with Denny McLain, Roberto Clemente, Micky Mantle, Al Kaline and the rest of my baseball cards. Manny Tankin stood outside the still open front door, afraid to venture into the house.

I hopped into the front seat. It was as hot as the back. Sweat poured down my face as I attempted to open Hippo's heavy door by holding the handle in one hand and banging on it with the other and kicking it again and again and again and again, but it wouldn't open.

Mrs. Why snatched up the telephone and dialed Mr. Why's number at work. The phone rang. She shouted into the phone. Manny, still standing in the doorway, looked out at the flowers again.

Upon answering the phone, Mr. Why turned very white. At the time, he was working in the State Attorneys General Office and had prosecuted several members of the mob. Various threats had been made, all very hush-hush, not suitable for the dinner table talk, so, instead, we all discussed the sameness of our days and Mrs. Why pretended nothing of the sort had happened.

I sat up tall and held the black steering wheel in my hands and drove in my mind's eye through the parking lot. I raced past a place I dubbed The Stinky Plant and into the world of smokestack silhouettes, and the soon-to-be broken-down city. In my imagination, I drove following the directions of my moods, making purposeful turns onto roads named Lane, Stone, and Drive, past pizza parlors, past police barracks, past mansions and playgrounds, libraries and museums.

Manny Tankin, tired of standing at the door and not wanting to participate in a sin of omission, climbed into Stego, revved its engine, and drove down the sidewalk in search of me. His legs chugged toward Cobbler's Field, where we never played because the big kids played there.

I, on the other hand, followed old trolley tracks past where mothers carried freshly baked bread home to their families in brown paper bags and older boys held their younger brother's hands or pulled them through the streets in red wagons.

While sitting in Stego, Manny watched the big kids play and finally mustered up enough courage to approach them and ask each if he had seen me: Donnie Broke, "No." Jimmie Hoodie. "No." Andy Arnold. "No Siree, Bob." Finally, Stewie Makepiece.

Stewie Makepiece couldn't really be trusted and everyone in the neighborhood knew it. It was rumored he had once been taken to Mayview for psychiatric testing and given electroshock therapy. That's why he had the lazy eye and was forever licking his lips and lying. Stewie Makepiece, tall and shifty, a red head with ratty eyes, looked down on Manny Tankin and said, "Yes," he had seen me that morning and "who in hell's fire wanted pray tell to know?"

I drove past my elementary school, Winthrop, built into a steep incline by some magical feat of engineering. I passed a vacant middle school waiting to be torn down because I imagined all of the students had fallen out of it. I yelled "Hi" to the high school and waved at its mascot, a furry cartoon out-of-proportion tiger who waved back at me and directed traffic. Hippo raced down long hills and into small towns of uninterrupted gray.

Stewie Makepiece stood beside Manny Tankin on our front steps as if to verify his account. Mrs. Why, phone in one hand, was not smiling. "Yes," Stewie had seen me before the birds were up even, before the sun was in the sky, before the morning air created its own eerie light. "Oh yes," Stewie Makepiece had seen me step from the sidewalk and get into an automobile—a black automobile. "For sure," he had seen this, cross his heart and hope for Heaven. "Yes," this was the truth, the absolute truth and nothing but…

No matter what part of the city I passed, retired steel workers with worn faces and tired eyes rocked away steadily on their front porches, waiting for their pension checks in same way they waited for their grandchildren to visit—grandchildren who now lived in the suburbs and embraced trendy malls that twinkled like Christmas all year round. There was talk that the pension checks might stop coming, and this made the old men very nervous.

"A big, black automobile," Mrs. Why said into the telephone while Stewie and Manny shifted from foot-to-foot on our front stoop. "What kind, Stewie?"

"I don't know," Makepiece said. "All I know is that the automobile black, old and ugly."

My mother said, "All the kid knows is it was big." Mrs. Why held her tongue when the police officer on the other end of the line asked if she had looked in all of the closets, if perhaps I had wondered into one of the neighbor's yards, if she had checked everywhere. Then, she panicked, imagining me lying face down in any number of outdoor swimming pools.

The police issued a standard statement, said, "They would alert all cars to be on the look-out."

Like Mr. Why, I clicked on the radio, which always worked even when the car was parked. I ran through several channels of static until I swear I heard a newsman say, "And a missing boy, Jayson Why, believed to be kidnapped. Be on the lookout for…" Then, in a deep voice, he described me perfectly like he was looking at a Polaroid. Was the whole city looking for me? And there I was sweating bullets, sitting in Hippo, holding onto the steering wheel, unable to open the door, which I kicked again for good measure and...

By now, Mrs. Why was frantic, waiting by the phone in the kitchen nook for a call from the kidnappers asking for ransom. She thought she would give anything, but what did we have? The house? The old car? No, not the car?

Mr. Why took long gulps from a water fountain, a wave cresting toward his lips before venturing outside. Other attorneys in black suits huddled around him wearing frightened faces.

I'd read about old man Carnegie from Steel City, frightened of Hell because of his exploitation of the working class, who believed those who died rich, thus died disgraced and Carnegie had tried to buy his way into Heaven by financing the building of museums and public libraries. If one looked closely enough at the old men who rocked away in every part of the city, you would see tired eyes; eyes that didn't see the automobile factories anymore; limbs that seldom ventured through museum doors; tired arms that never brought home books.

I was terribly thirsty, but I had stopped sweating. In my mind's eye, Hippo raced down one-way streets, over cobblestones, past churches, turned corners, turned curves, stopped in front of bone orchards. The Stinky Plant was still pouring out its stink. The factories were still working overtime. I maneuvered onto a road I named Distance.

Manny Tankin peddled past Jungle Gym Park,

around the spinning upside-down ride on the look-out for some sign of me. Although no one was on the rides, the carousel with the metal rails and the clowns spun round and round. He jumped the curb and valiantly moved Stego out into the middle of the street.

I tried to roll down the driver-side window, but it only moved two inches and then stuck.

A line of cars stretched long and hard behind Stego —impatient drivers, knuckle-white, bemused and exasperated, laid on their horns and at the same time didn't want to startle the little boy into any sudden moves.

Stewie Makepiece kicked up dirt in my front yard and smiled. For once in his life, an adult had believed him.

As Hippo turned onto Distance, Stego, armor plated, suddenly appeared with Manny behind the wheel pedaling in blind fury toward me. Size diminished through heat as Hippo surged forward with a start. Manny and I locked eyes. Right before we crashed head-on, Hippo's doors opened, became willowy wings, and the car leapt into the air and flew toward the tentacled clouds.

And then everything stopped. The newsman's voice turned to static and the heat shot up in waves against the pavement. The world of steel melted away, and Hippo's windshield shattered. There was a kind of purging, a pounding in my ears like the sound of a searing, blaring horn, and no matter how many times I pressed the center of the steering wheel, the sound, tinny and far off, wouldn't leave my head. And, the whole day swelled backwards and forwards in slow motion. I saw the flash of Stego swerve into me and felt myself jumping out of myself and the seat as my head cracked into a transparent windshield. I can see this happening with such clarity and marveled how the body secures such ingenious ways to protect itself.

Both cars sat in the intersection, askew, utterly wrecked, damaged in ways that could never be put back together. Like the city, they hadn't yet crumbled but sat there— static—waiting for time and tow trucks to take them away.

And, suddenly I came to myself and saw them all: Tar, Hippo, Stego, abandoned, sitting in a junkyard, whose piles of scrap metal lay crushed and on top of each other like broken and sad, crushed faces, waiting, for what? To turn to rust? And then to dust? And then to be picked up and scattered by the wind? Or, like the sound of an electric window shade being pulled upward from somewhere above by unseen hands…

To his credit, Mr. Why had not panicked when he found me unconscious from the heat. He did panic, however, when he couldn't open the door. He beat on the windows of The Hipposaurus and watched as the world—suddenly collapsed by heat and blind decisions, by emptiness and sudden losses, by an enfolding of time—came into focus: All the kids were grouped in a five o'clock clump gathered together in the far reaches of our lawn, the football's emerging spiral separating itself from Al Kaline's branches and the ball fell into my outstretched hands and then I fell to the ground. I felt the neighborhood's crushing weight, unable to breath, unable to speak, wanting to shout, "It's my ball. I caught it. I get to hand the ball back to dad. I get to call the next play…"

Two firm hands lifted me up out of the pile—and suddenly, the world had come for us, as it eventually would find a way to collide with us all.

Exhausted by his futile search, Manny Tankin pulled into his driveway, considered parking Stego in its usual place in the garage, but he left it outside. He was in an awful hurry to talk with his mother.

There were tears in my father's eyes when he finally opened the passenger side door of The Hipposaurus, carefully extricated me from behind the wheel, walked purposefully through the heavy glass doors and carried me up all three flights of stairs. By the time he had entered his office, my eyes, Thank God, had fluttered open. He bought me a cold drink, told me to sit still awhile, to catch my breath, to stop moving.

Mrs. Why sobbed into the mouthpiece when she heard the news.

Mr. Tankin, on his way to work, accidentally backed up over Manny's truck later that morning.

Mr. Why drove us home through what felt like a deserted city, back over familiar streets with strange names I had never heard of…

Stewie Makepiece kicked up some dirt and ran to his mailbox to get the mail for his father.

In less than a week, my father drove me through the hazy morning steamy light of the city in a red Cutlass

1968 hardtop. It was new and sporty, and my father had never had anything like it. We named it "Cutler" for short.

His old car, the black Plymouth Valiant, The Hipposaurus, Hippo, had dissolved into tears when the tow truck operator came and my father paid the man five dollars to take it away. There's something sad in a car like an abandoned life that doesn't deserve payment in the end, and I remember wondering if paying to take Hippo away was something he had done to honor the car or something he had done to help him forget it.

As we drove Cutler through the city, flowers were left for the old men who rocked away on their front porches, alone, but no one needed to tell me or them where all of the factories had gone because we knew the world had come for them, too.

THE BOOK OF WHY

In 1965, I was a television addict. I made weekly schedules, and my sister and I fought not only over the programs we watched but for the best view of the tube–plunking down right in front of the TV, elbows resting on the ginormous throw pillows directly in front of the screen. For me it was *Green Acres, Petticoat Junction,* and *Family Affair*—although Mr. French creeped me out. My sister went in for *Captain Kangaroo* in the mornings, *That Girl* (when she could), and *Cool McCool* on weekends with Snoopy, Jenny, Countdown, and Scooter. My father watched *Mission Impossible, The Smothers Brothers,* and the last season of *Perry Mason*—who reminded me so much of my father that the show unsettled me. My mother, if she watched at all, tuned into the nightly news. She said Cronkite reminded her of her great grandfather.

I was also the self-proclaimed television schedule-maker and enforcer. I worked the weekly schedule into a piece of refrigerator art–each line highlighted. For reliable sources, I used the *TV Guide* cross-referenced with two local newspapers. I was as meticulous as I was ruthless. There were penalties for missing an appointed viewing. For my sister, there was to be no milk on her cereal (for coming late to the tube), or in more egregious cases, the forced preparation of a liver dinner with my mother (who only cooked the stuff when my father was out of town); or, finally, the penance of doing good for being bad: giving one of her many dolls to the Little Sisters of the Poor (if she didn't show up for her appointed viewing at all). For my father, the punishments needed to be subtle in that he couldn't know about them. (It was his television after all!) I had to let him think that he was suffering an interminable amount of bad luck (like when he lost his keys, misplaced his wallet, couldn't find his necktie, pulled off the buttons on his shirt, or bit his tongue while eating his diner), and I hoped against hope his lucklessness would prey on his conscience and that eventually he would come to believe he might have done something to get cross-wise with the universe. When that "what-the-heck" quizzical look appeared on his face, I would remind him of the many times he'd signed up for and then either forgotten, found himself otherwise busy (and this was always with work), or fully refused to fulfill his television watching obligations.

I was subtle.

My father would look at me unbelievingly, and then, I believed, hang his head in shame.

My mother, a very pragmatic woman, a mathematician, was more interested in the components of my schedule than watching any of the shows on TV, save the news. She hoped, I believed, I would follow in her mathematical footsteps and one day help create three-dimensional schedules for the airlines or buses. She told me, there was money to be made in scheduling: "Money for the wonderful and wise, Jayson," she said; "money for the all-knowing and powerful."

In the family, my obsession came to be known as "THE SCHEDULE," and everyone (especially my sister) uttered those two words with disdain.

THE SCHEDULE, as I said, I felt compelled to tack up on the refrigerator *and* to tape a copy to each of the bathroom mirrors. (Everyone could see it there, right?)

THE SCHEDULE, I'll admit, was as righteous as it was obnoxious.

I put all of my research and preliminary notes into a ledger book (with metal rings in the top left corner) that my mother bought me and that I called THE BOOK OF WHY. I filled its many pages with colored pencil illustrations (of me smashing my toy car into Manny Tankin's toy car or working in the hole the hardhats left on Winsome Street with Rocky Bottoms or riding down through The Netherlands on my bike behind Kate Wheeler). These illustrations made up my younger world, however, the rest of my ledger was filled with extensive and meticulous research and notes in preparation for making the final large-scale refrigerator version of THE SCHEDULE.

I even carried THE BOOK OF WHY to school, so I could work on drafting and redrafting a mini-mock-up of THE SCHEDULE during my free time, in study hall, and later even during class. (My mantra was: don't wallpaper the house until you've wallpapered the closet.) My teachers thought I was dutifully taking notes, and, at first, left me alone, half-believing they had a scholar in their midst. Soon they came to find I couldn't answer any of their questions and barely knew what they were talking about–their voices a droning, dull, background hum.

I loved leafing through THE BOOK OF WHY'S pages, especially at night when the house was quiet, except for the moan of the furnace. I'd carefully turn each page, admiring my drawings and trying to imprint its notes into my DNA.

We had a huge spider-like TV antenna that thumped on the roof. From my bedroom on the second floor, it sounded as if there were deer up there running in all directions. The thump, thump, thump was rather comforting, and I liked being able to turn a dial down in the living room and affect something on the roof. I imagined the antenna was a huge eyeball overseeing everything. And, there was much bad in the world: assassinations, civil rights violence, the Vietnam War Show, and strong men everywhere.

The evening news anchors echoed the MIGHT-MAKES-RIGHT attitude of Imperialism; yet, it seemed to me that the world had already decided on apathy. Apathy, not empathy, not compassion, not peace. In the end, the purpose of television was to keep us watching, constantly watching, half-paying attention. To keep us all in an apathetic dream state or an angry malaise, directed at everyone except ourselves.

School had always been an anathema for me—I am not ashamed to say that I hated it. I relished Friday nights because of the two free days to follow, and I hated the sound of the ticking clock on Sunday evenings. I loved summer vacations and could never understand those who waited with anticipation and glee for school to begin.

One day in class, I had enough of the snide remarks from my teachers and I just snapped. I turned off. I think it was because I was watching too much television; and, let's face it, under the signal, under the static, under the mesmerizing images on the screen, television pretends to mirror real life, but the problem, of course, was when the line began to blur.

There I was one moment—my BOOK OF WHY open—scratching away, making corrections, attempting to make the perfect schedule that would ensure that everything would turn out okay, that my sister would admire me, that my father would come home from work on time, that my mother would pay attention to me—was any of this too much to ask? Apparently so, and the next moment I turned into static. My world became insular. I found myself transformed: one part knowing what I was doing, the other part watching and waiting for television's tidy conclusions so that I could go out in the world and find my way into an uncertain future toward what I hoped was a predestined ending.

Around the same time, I became fascinated by the television show *Dark Shadows*—a soap opera about a lonely vampire, the existential Barnabus Collins, whose eyes glowed. I loved the characters Maggie Collins, Willie Loomis, and Dr. Julia Hoffman. Barnabus wanted to be cured, to embrace humanity, to face the consequences of his past decisions. The show was broadcast in black and white and took place in Collingwood. Barnabus didn't appear until the sixth episode, and I loved when the character Willie Loomis ventured into a dark room and saw Barnabus' chained coffin. Then, Barnabus' hand reached out of the coffin and grabbed Willie's throat. I was hooked. I loved the tone: the painting of Barnabus' portrait, the castle, his unrequited love for Josette du Pres. *Dark Shadows* had it all: the stylistics, the characters, adventure and danger, the dangerous adventure, and the passing of a bygone age right in front of you (with 60s dancing, hairstyles and clothes). I believed that if *I* just reached out that I could grab and hold onto it.

After I turned into static, I began skipping school under one pretense or another so that I could watch *Dark Shadows*. I was worried that Maggie Evans, who had been bitten by Barnabus, would not regain her health. And, at first—and I doubt that she ever believed me—my mother put up with my stomach aches, my general malaise, my flu-like symptoms, and my ear aches. (Note that whatever I said was wrong with me was not something that anyone could literally see.)

Then, Maggie went missing. I wanted to find her and at the same time I wanted to disappear like her (albeit not into a sanitarium). I wanted, like Barnabus Collins, to be able to stay up all night. Perhaps the night was my place. I watched in fascination: the experiments on Barnabus, the dream curse, werewolves and ghosts. I missed day-after-day of school and didn't feel like I was really missing anything—and, in my own mind, I wasn't.

During this time, THE BOOK OF WHY took on larger than life proportions. It's hard to explain but writing in my book–making lists, doing research for THE SCHEDULE became a kind of anchor for me—a habit with its cues and its rewards.

Late, late at night, I would find my favorite pen, open THE BOOK OF WHY and get to work. Find my way into the inside—something I knew and didn't know as well as I wanted to. There were eternal questions beyond my presupposed answers: eternal revisions that could go on forever if I wanted them to, if I let them, and during the day, there was *Dark Shadows*—traveling to 1795, 1897, 1969, 1995.

It was then that my mother caught me. In a rare and arrogant move, I'd attempted to offer proof of my illness feigning a temperature by dipping it into a cup of warm water. My mother surprised me.

"Jayson Why, what in the world?"

"Hey, Mom, I was just . . ."

"What were you doing with that thermometer?"

My mother, exasperated at my inability to answer any of her questions, grabbed THE BOOK OF WHY and began examining the pages as if the answers to all her questions were written there.

"My temperature's 102," I said.

"Don't fudge numbers, Jayson. That's a sin."

"I wasn't." I took a swig of hot water from the cup, and it was so hot I spit it out all over her.

"Why is that water so hot?" she said. "Let me see the thermometer."

She shook it down in her hand, took the cup from my hand, and dipped it into the water.

"102.6! What in the world?"

"I'm sorry, Mom. I. . ."

To say my mother hit the roof is an understatement. Thank God she had an aversion to violence. I leave you to imagine the continued stammering and stuttering—the muted and nonsensical explanations when my mother continually pointed to the cup of warm water and alternatingly to my thermometer.

"Ma, please."

"102.6! You better not say anything else, Jayson. Why, Not a solitary single word. Don't even try. Don't make me count to ten before you find yourself in your room for the rest of your bygone days. I can't even begin to know what your father will say and do."

"I was. . .I am . . .If only I could find a way of telling the truth without anyone knowing what actually happened," I quoted *Dark Shadows*.

"Not a word, Jayson. Not another word, ever. And no TV either."

"You're taking my soul away from me."

The television was immediately snapped off—Barnabus' head dissolved in front of my eyes into a white dot. The world of color found my cheeks. With the TV switch turned off, it was as if another world was turned on, and, I must say, I didn't like it.

THE BOOK OF WHY was taken away from me. The television was taken away. THE SCHEDULE was taken down from the fridge and all of the bathroom mirrors. Everyone watched what they wanted on television, and from my perspective there was no order in the house. For my mother, the house's order had been restored.

I remember one late night, I was locked in my room, and I heard the antennae thumping on the roof. There outside and framed by my window was Barnabas Collins. He was staring in at me. I tried to adjust this picture, to reach out toward the static, to see the future, to live happily ever. "You've made a very serious mistake, Jayson Why. Your foolish curiosity has not brought you into my bleak universe." I found myself looking into Barnabus' glowing eyes long after the narrator said, "And that for as long as they lived, the dark shadows at Collinwood were but a memory of the distant past."

SWIMMING FOR FOSSILS

I have my theories about the summer we were swimming for fossils. That summer was the hottest I can remember. So hot was the ground that digging a hole couldn't cool a soul; so hot were the top layers of the earth that they festered like cinders buried deep under skin; so mixed with tattered earth were the beetles and dried worms that each morning's appearance of these earthy creatures filled me with questions.

The living lay inert. Squirrels held fast to telephone wires, their bushy tails curling up like question marks punctuating humming conversations. Our family dog, a short-haired collie named Ransom, didn't have the energy to bark and lay like a misplaced doorstop, thrown out in the middle of the yard, covered in leaves. The birds, we thought, were stuffed: they were so quiet, they merely stared at the ground. Fat bumblebees fell asleep in flower beds, motionless in crushed pollen-centers.

And those things that should have been still were in motion.

The leaves swirled like dust storms without wind's reason. Tree trunks swayed to the musical heat. Winsome Street rippled and buckled—a sticky black river in front of my parents' house, glistening from curb to gutter. Throughout the day, the sun mixed tar at its leisure, its yellow eye overseeing the thickness of the broth.

And, as day moved into afternoon, the houses that lined Winsome Street in misplaced rows began to cry: their windows, eyes; their shutters, eyelashes—and, through their open doors, they began to beg.

Day upon day, this upheaval played out on the surface of the world, and any manner of motionlessness or motion, begging or tears neither cooled nor pacified the ground.

By early evening, the members of the silent aviary, feathered and forlorn, too drowsy to return to their nests, stood sideways on light poles; bumblebees hid, their sticky legs clinging to the undersides of flowers; squirrels hung upside down in twilight's balance, their tails hooked to telephone wires; and, lightning bugs beamed, perpetually on high.

At bedtime, the moon crept perilously close to my window, bathing me in surreal light while surrendering up a slide show: I watched through the screen that was my bedroom window as the ground split open, revealing layers of grief; stones stacked and sheered, reflected moonlight in random shades of red; tree roots, cut off at their core, exposed the tenuousness of life; and beetles of all sorts scurried about making purposeful plans.

Each morning, after breakfast, Rocky Bottoms, my neighbor, who lived in a very flat two-story structure across Winsome Street, and I would meet on the sidewalk in front my house. In one hand, Rocky would be carrying Benny Goodfurnuttin', his pet hamster, in a gilded cage and his 'Terry Tetradactyl' lunchbox in the other. I would be carrying two unopened umbrellas in one hand and my 'Ronny Rex' lunchbox in the other. The umbrellas were my mother's idea, who preached that one should be prepared for all possible outcomes rain or shine and whose sleepy head surfaced behind our front window after I walked out the door each morning. I could feel her and Rocky's mother watching us, not so much concerned where we were going, perhaps, but where we might end up.

Together, umbrellas, lunchboxes and Benny's cage in our hands, we'd pretend to make our way toward Jungle Gym Park, with its metal slides, its rusted swings, its torturous and twisted igloo-like girded stanchions, its tilt-a-wheel, whose miniature clowns either spun in endless circles or sat menacingly still. The clowns scared the crap out of Rocky, who, as we approached the Park, would talk soothingly to Benny, and tell him everything would be okay, forever and always.

Soon, however, when we were sure that our mother's faces had left their respective windows, we would circle back toward our houses, trudging down Winsome Street, looking out for cars, and side-stepping the fresh, sticky tar.

The PIT, a square, dark tar-filled hole, set off by yellow tape and orange cones that workman had recently cut into Winsome Street, sat directly across from my house, but was mercifully shadowed by a large oak tree, whose branches shielded us from the roaming eyes of our mothers.

Punctuated by the sun's morning rays, I'd hold out the umbrellas' metal tips, my arm covering their lengths, and Rocky would choose: the one holding the longest of the two was left with the luck. Then, together, we'd teeter at the edge of the PIT, synchronize the openings of our umbrellas, and parachute down, down, down—our feet sinking in the air until our eyes were level with the ground.

Once underground, we would use our already opened umbrellas to shield our bodies from the curious woolly mammoths that occasionally rumbled by and let out squawks—the horn sirens swirling around the pit long after the cars had breezed by.

Rocky carefully set Benny Goodfurnuttin's gilded cage beside us. We placed our clean folded clothes into thin piles outside the PIT, put our shoes on top of the piles, and placed our lunch boxes beside them. Then, we would liberate our hardened armor from the garbage bag left overnight in the PIT and proceed to equip our legs with tar-stiffened pants, our feet with plastic knee-high boots, and our mid-sections with filthy long-sleeved summer windbreakers. We would cover our heads with baseball caps, whose creased bills shielded our faces, collapse our umbrellas, and tuck the bottoms of our pants into our boots.

"Swimming for Fossils," was an intricate game in which we attempted to pull what was above ground below and put what was below ground above. We had a rule book and everything with 10 rules and an addendum.

Rule # 1: Only the Dead need apply.

Rule #2: All rocks, fossils, shells, petroglyphs and even things that look like rocks, fossils, shells, and petroglyphs welcome.

Rule # 3: No animals of any kind allowed [except for Benny] (i.e., the living need not apply).

Rule # 4: All items found in the PIT stayed in the PIT.

Rule #5: Point values are awarded to finder:

> Rocks (1)
> Dead Worms and beetles (2)
> Shells (3)
> Fossils (4)
> Petroglyphs (5)

[All other items are subject to an average of both proposed scores for inter-rater reliability. We've learned this concept in 6th grade science from Mr. Kenny.]

Rule #6: No swearing, fighting or hullabaloo in the PIT.

[Mr. Bottoms used words like hullabaloo and

ballyhoo all the time and we looked them up—as in "Rocky stop you're ballyhooing immediately!]

Rule #7: Conduct oneself like a proper anthropologist at all times.

Rule #8: Create a classification system (see # 5). A careful typology (Again, Mr. Kenny).

Rule #9: What goes down in the PIT stays in the PIT forever and swear to Cuthbert, even if mothers' ask or try to bribe with an extra scoop of vanilla ice cream on store bought pies.

Rule #10: Hang or display all items against the side of the PIT/tallying each with an appropriate hashmark using chalk stolen from Mr. Bottom's workroom.

Addendum: Anyone who finds this journal must bury it on the right side of the old oak tree.

In the PIT that summer we found an old three-cornered hat (3 points); rusted pipes (2 points a piece); a championship track and field card featuring Walter Bursch from 1910 (5 points); the cylinder for an Ad Conklin self-filling fountain pen (4 points); a tar stained Reader's Digest featuring an article on life way down deep in the ocean (3 points); a three-pronged fork (1 point), a steering wheel (4 points); three rusted cans of Coke (1 point a piece) and a broken welding helmet with a strap (invaluable and incalculable each of us took turns wearing it).

And into the PIT we pulled dead beetles: devil's coach horse beetles, stag beetles, cowboy beetles, whirligig and blister beetles, powder post beetles, long-horn beetles, carpet and Emerald Ash Borers (each 2 points). And earth worms (pigeic, edogeic, and anecic—complements of Mr. Kenny's fantastic teaching, if he ever finds this journal upon our demise, REMEMBER TO BURY IT UNDER THE OLD OAK TREE.)

Rocky and I at first used the tips of our umbrellas to strike hash marks until the tips became too sharp and we took to using big blocks of chalk liberated from Mr. Bottoms' workroom. We made two separate columns—"Above" and "Below."

At noon, we'd unlatch our lunch boxes and eat giganotosaurus sandwiches, drink pond water from our thermoses, and feed Benny Goodfurnuttin' sunflower seeds, which he'd malevolently spit back at us, eyeing, instead, the dead beetles we'd pulled into the PIT. At the end of the meal, we'd pick our teeth with well-preserved pterodactyl bones. (Somehow my mother had thought of everything, even toothpicks.)

Late afternoon when the lid of the big eye began to close, Rocky and I would tally the results. The loser would have to climb out of the PIT and undress under the branches of the oak tree, racing the time-switch, which for some reason activated the streetlights at 5. The winner would stay in the PIT with Benny and then leisurely climb out of his armor, carefully maneuver it into the plastic bag, and bless it with the longer of the two umbrellas.

Then, while standing on the sidewalk holding the umbrellas and our lunch boxes and Benny's cage and looking innocent, we would shake hands on a job well-done and say we could never lose on Winsome street.

Holding the closed umbrellas, Ronnie Rex and I would enter through the garage, tiptoe past the tangled fishing equipment, give a nod to dormant model train set, eye the Coke bottles wearing metal derbies all lined up on rusty metal shelves and silently spring up the two-step.

Creeping forward on my hands and knees, if necessary, I'd expertly avoid my mother. Once safe and in the bathroom, I'd scrub down with Lava—the only soap effective in removing tar—and enter the kitchen where inevitably my mother with a dish towel draped over her forearm would be setting places for dinner, and I'd smile because I was as squeaky-clean as the plates on the table.

Approvingly, my mother would pour me an iced-cold glass of Wink soda pop, and in the few moments before my father came home, together, we would indulge in what she affectionately called a "Winkie Break." Mom would tell me about her fantastic day battling giant two-headed ants and chasing after ginormous dust bunnies with the nozzle of her Hoover, and I would lie about umbrella trips to the sun and full loops around the rusted steepled swing-set and recount conversations with the clowns (who said things that sounded like "Who Ha!" and "Whoey! Whoey! Whoey!" and "Fascination Alligator" as they spun in circles in Jungle Gym Park.

At 6:15 p.m. on the dot, my father's beat-up Plymouth Valiant would slither into our gravel drive, and soon after, my father, with briefcase in hand, suit jacket slung over his shoulder, and flip-down sunglasses that made him look like a mobster on vacation would grow like a marigold through the garage, over the two-step, around the living room and into the kitchen.

Dinner! Then television, if I was lucky, then bed, where I would lie under my Ford Mustang bedspread with my eyes wide open until the moon peered in through the window. Soon after, the ground gurgled and heaved, and the slide show began: flatfooted demons holding my umbrellas tossed oily moonlit skins into the PIT.

One late afternoon in August, quite suddenly and without warning, Benny Goodfurnuttin' somehow found a way out of his cage. We watched in horror as Benny's tiny hooves moved in slow-motion sinking into the tar at the bottom of the PIT. Benny, who continued to sink down bit-by-bit, looked at us as if it was our fault that he was there, which it was. Rocky panicked and reached down too quickly in an effort to rescue Benny, but, in a terrible moment of miscalculation, Rocky's head banged hard against the side of the PIT, which made a hollow sound reviving the dead worms and beetles that suddenly wriggled and twisted against its walls. Rocky's body collapsed onto the razor tip of the longest umbrella. Tar rushed out of his mouth like a frozen scream, and then all was silent. The seconds ticked by as day began its sticky retreat, and then the sky began to mirror the tar river below. The moon's faint outline was in the sky, and I realized it had been there all along with the sun, not melting in the incredible heat—not fading away.

Mom answered my insistent banging on our door.

"Oh, how could you, Jayson?" she said looking at the tar-covered clothes. "No, Sir! You just stand there where you are! Go ahead, turn around so you can enjoy the view. It's the only picture of the outside you're going to be seeing for a long time. And don't even think about running. In fact, don't move a muscle until your father pulls into that driveway. I don't know what we're going to do with those clothes. Burn them, I guess."

"Rocky's hurt," I yelled. "He fell in the PIT."

"What PIT?" mother said.

"The PIT! Out in the street," I pointed. "Rocky hit his head and then fell."

In a strange turn of events, my father's car suddenly slid into the driveway. The ground hummed beneath his feet, electrically, and then the streetlights kicked on one-by-one and the front windows of the houses that lined Winsome Street flicked on, too. Fireflies became significant dots of light, and I realized that they, too, like the moon, had been there all the time, but for some reason, like the moon lacked significance in daylight. There was a rumbling, a shaking and then a loud groaning. Tar rushed out of the ground and threatened to freeze my feet in place. My father raced toward his car, Rocky's limp hands and feet were hanging over the cradle formed by his arms. Stiff black shadows that must have been Rocky's parents slid past me and into my father's Valiant soon en route to the hospital.

In the quiet garage, I took off my tar-stiffened clothes, which lay on the floor beside the Coke bottles whose metal derbies presided over what looked like a fallen comrade, an invisible boy whose shape still filled the cloth.

When I got out of the shower, my pajamas were pressed flat against my bed. I opened them and held them up to me wondering how long it would take for them to take on my shape.

This time when the moon crept close instead of just lying there looking at the screen that was my window, I forced myself out of bed, opened my window and crawled out over the ledge. As I made my way through the window frame, my eyes opened: the moon was close working its light together with the streetlights to illuminate the night. The underground appeared to be coming up from below: fossils everywhere, spit-up from the depths: trace fossils, body fossils, the strata of rock, shells, petrification and preserved remains—compressed beetles, flies, mosquitos, snails, cicadas, gastropods, ammonites and trilobites, fossils everywhere, scattered around the PIT. I made my way toward its edge, the bottoms of my feet crunching against the dirt. I looked down in the PIT and saw the cage. I held my nose and plunged down, down without the umbrella to break my fall. While standing at the bottom, I touched the walls, my fingers tracing the hashmarks. I tried to pick up my feet fearing that I would trample on Benny. I couldn't find him anywhere and for a moment panicked until I heard him chirp;

there he was scurrying around inside of his cage, okay. I thanked God and I looked over at Rocky's silent house, and imagined that I could be forgiven in some imagined future…

And, now, I am a thirty-year-old-shadow standing in the afternoon of what used to be my yard with a one-handed digging tool. Sinking through layers of tar and time, rocks and shells, dead worms and beetles as the moon moves busily about somewhere above me. I look for the old journal, whose purple cover lights up my imagination in recurring dreams. I dig and dig and when I can't find it, I sit under the tree and look at the windows of Rocky's house for a moment.

"Well, well, if it isn't Jayson Why, come back to visit us! Come in, Jayson! Come in. Plop right down any old where. Can I get you something to drink?" Mrs. Bottoms said. She looks tired and her eye-creased smile betrays her.

"He looks like he needs a stiff lemonade," Rocky's father, older, clothes creased, says.

"Would you like a lemonade, Jayson?" his mother says over the clinking of ice cubes.

"Jayson, you'll never guess what I found in my workshop while I was summer-searching for things I misplaced during the winter. Usually I don't find more than a few pennies or stray buttons. Funny you showed up, though, because just yesterday, I found a box of slides. Those were the days of slide projectors, Jayson, when you could point your camera at something and that world would later appear on the screen. Do you remember?" Mr. Bottoms says.

"Of course, he doesn't remember. He was just a child. How could he remember?"

Mr. Bottoms is already plugging in an old slide projector after expending a great deal of effort untangling its cord. Mrs. Bottoms flicks the light switches in tandem and white light forms a perfect square against the wall.

Slide 1: A blurry slide of their weeping house.

Slide 2: The oak tree that stretched forever upward toward the sun. Birds were sitting on telephone wires, and a squirrel's tail rose up in a question mark between them.

Slide 3: "Now here's one of Winsome Street. Funny how the ripples seemed to make the street move," Mr. Bottoms says. "Well, in those days it did move, didn't it, Jayson? In those days the earth forgot its manners. Sometimes if you crept up on it off-guard, you might catch it in motion. Isn't that right? Isn't that how it was?"

Slide 4: "Remember when the two of you used to go out and play in that hole the workmen men had left in the street after working on some-such under the ground? Of course you remember. How could any of us ever forget. There you are! Look how guilty you both look!" Mrs. Bottoms says.

"We're so glad that you came back, Jayson."

And I would have liked to say: "Yes, I think, I am a better person now than I was then. At least I tell myself that and would like to believe it." But, I didn't say anything.

I'll admit that such indecision has followed me throughout life although, at first, I knew I had done the right thing by Rocky. I had sought help and weathered the deep, disappointed stares of my mother and my father. My failure was in my inability to follow-through.

What, I ask myself to this day, had Rocky and I hoped to find in the PIT? Was it that we mattered? Was it that we wished to turn the past over in our hands and examine it? And what in those summer days had we tried to offer up?

I wish I could say that it all worked out for the best between Rocky and me, but, of course, anyone who has lived for even a day knows that's not always the way things go.

Rocky lost his spleen, but survived and Winsome Street became an unimaginable gulf between us—like a gap between historical ages. We used to walk to school together, but as far as I can remember, we never did again.

In the last slide, Rocky and I are standing together in my front yard. I'm not looking at Rocky, although I look like I want to. I wonder who is holding the camera. It must have been his father capturing that moment.

Yes, I have my theories about the summer we were swimming for fossils.

One theory is that Rocky Bottoms and I are still in that PIT talking to each other like the conversations that hum through the telephone lines, like the tar-covered clothes we used to leave in the plastic bag.

A second theory is that Rocky is hiding behind his shuttered windows waiting for me to come on up to his room like a daylight firefly so we can shake hands and take the leap together and finally examine the clockwork below in plain daylight, to turn the past over in our hands and examine it, to study it, to make it all matter so we won't have to carry the thoughts of it in our dreams.

THE DAY THE END OF THE WORLD WAS AT HAND

"I've signed you up for swimming lessons at the Y.M.C.A. Lessons start Monday. That's tomorrow," Mother said as I stood on pretty pink petals that lined the ground of our backyard jungle. A late spring snow had just left the rooftop of our home. The gutters were filled with brown, wet leaves. Father stood high atop a wooden ladder. Looking up, I saw his blue jeans and the dirty soles of his shoes. Mother stood under him, holding the bottom rungs. She wore a small bee-hive hairdo, a plaid shirt, and black slacks. Every so often a clump of leaves exploded in a burst behind me.

In those days, Father was a dominant shadow, whose late-afternoon appearances signified dinner and whose morning appearances signified weekend. Mother was someone whose presence I always felt and who seemed hell-bent on telling me what to do.

In those days, I spent my Easter morning break watching *The Mickey Mouse Club* on television and most of my afternoons playing army in our backyard jungle. There was a war on, and I was Sergeant-Major-Corporal-Minor-Jayson Why, Dog-of-War, Enemy-to-all-Enemies. "Destruction" was my middle name: I knocked the heads off of weeds and wildflowers with plastic golf clubs, dug deep trenches toward the center of the earth with sandbox shovels, and buried myself under leaves, camouflaging exposed limbs with parts of bushes. Happily, I made booby traps out of Mother's clotheslines, lured neighborhood kids into my backyard jungle, and laughed myself wet when Father's underwear sprang up at them like one-eyed monsters, and they ran screaming home. I tried to change what I could. I tried to understand what I couldn't. There was a war on.

In those days, I hadn't yet learned to swim, and Kenny Bloom, my next-door neighbor, was yet to go off to Vietnam. I'd convinced myself that if Vietnam hadn't happened, Kenny wouldn't have had to leave home at all.

In those days, I stood in my backyard jungle peeking through the brambles and pine needles at the Bloom's magical house. Somewhere in the middle of the huge expanse of grass between our houses, I gazed across the 17th parallel.

The Bloom's house didn't seem to belong to our neighborhood. It had everything: large, thick, white pillars that kept the roof from falling; a crooked walkway made out of bricks that wound a snake's path to the front door, and a real-honest-to-God doorbell one pulled with a rope. The Bloom's house reminded me of The White House, and Old Mr. Bloom a slightly fatter version of the president. He even had a crew cut and a rag-top Cadillac. I thought the Bloom's must have been very special indeed to have been blessed with such things.

And, somehow I knew we would never have the things that the Bloom's had: we had a tiny, red house with green shingles; a huge oak tree in our front lawn; and, red and yellow flowers neatly placed in window boxes; we had a light post in the corner of the yard that stretched far up into the sky and looked like it might fall on you at any moment, and a sign on the corner named Stop, but nobody ever did. Father owned a Plymouth Valiant with wide holes in the floorboards, and I owned a red Western Auto bicycle that leaned most days on its kickstand in our gravel drive. We didn't have big, white pillars holding up our house or a winding brick path that led to our front door; we didn't have a rag-top Cadillac or a real doorbell that chimed. We just didn't. We never would.

"Jayson! Did you hear me?" Mother repeated. "I've signed you up for swimming lessons at the Y.M.C.A. Lessons start tomorrow."

Kenny Bloom was going off to war, and I was starting swimming lessons at the Y.M.C.A.

The world just didn't seem right.

My eyes met Father's in a moment of magical understanding.

"Don't worry, Bud. You'll get through it," he said to me.

"I know, but you know," I said.

"I know, and you'll survive," he said.

I wasn't so sure.

I had only been to the Y.M.C.A. indoor pool once and had gazed up at the endless spaces in the ceiling—the girders crisscrossed in a network of angry thoughts. I had breathed in the green humid air and had felt warm and cold at the same time.

I looked away from my father and back to the Bloom's mysterious house. Through the branches and pine needles, it looked farther away than ever. The clouds had stopped moving; the world was still.

The front door opened and Kenny, handsome and tall, walked out of his house and stood high on top of the hill, wearing a T-shirt and holding a frisbee, which reached unheard-of heights as he waved goodbye. I burst out of the jungle chasing the frisbee's elongated shadow. I wanted to stop running, to wave back, but the frisbee sailed over my head, hovering above the street, spinning, going nowhere, and finally falling, meeting its shadow on the ground.

Kenny rushed by like the wind in his father's rag-top Cadillac, taking a spin around the neighborhood one last time. His mother sat beside him and his dog Topper barked into the spokes. Above the roar of the engine, the taillights lit up as the Caddy leaned into the corner, passed the tree in my front yard, passed the falling lamp post, passed my Western Auto bicycle, passed my father's Valiant, ran through STOP and disappeared.

The next day, the pool at the YMCA was filled with kids. I refused to get in the water and sat on the wide bench alone, watching them. They swam back and forth, their heads looking strange, bobbing on the surface. They waved for me to get in. Yelled the water's great. They waited, but I just looked down at my feet and stayed put on the bench.

Mother was very disappointed to hear I hadn't moved since she had left me on the bench and spent a long time talking to the high school kid who was supposed to teach me. He just shook his head, looked at me, shook his head again, and then looked down at his own bare feet. That night my father tried to smile at me over dinner but didn't seem to be able to.

After Kenny Bloom disappeared, I watched for him each night on television, but I never saw him, only a lot of soldiers who looked like him.

In August, my father came for me in his new red Cutlass 1968 hardtop. He was so proud of that car. It was sporty, and he'd never had anything like it before. In fact, I think that red Cutlass was the first thing my father felt he really owned and that included his house, and the land around it.

His old car, a black Plymouth Valiant, had recently become scrap metal, dissolving into tears when the tow truck operator came to take it away; my father paid the man five dollars. Before it was towed away, I ran out of the house and leapt into the backseat hoping that my father wouldn't get rid of it if I was still inside. There were tears in his eyes when he pulled open the side door and extended his hand.

Everything about the interior of the red Cutlass was new, except for the steering wheel—the only thing the old car had left us: a silver-capped horn that shone out-of-place as magnificently as a sheriff's badge on a modern policeman.

My mother's thin, disembodied hands disappeared before she could get the bay window open and wave goodbye; the Cutlass paused at the corner stop sign, and we moved clear out of sight.

The newness of the car was a part of the age I was living in where spaceships were no longer science fiction, where cars might soon be able to take-off into the air.

Its newness contrasted with my father, who'd had such a hard life that he was fond of telling me he had become old while still a boy.

In one photograph of him, he is twenty-five, standing tall amongst the other graduates of his law school class. In the picture he seems like he is breathing for the world: the first member of his family to graduate from high school, college, and now this.

While in law school, his father had died suddenly and that's how my father inherited the Valiant. He said when he turned the key to that car and all of the gages suddenly came to life, he realized his father was never coming back.

By the time I got to ride in the Valiant, though, it

was thoroughly rusted. There were holes in the floorboards, and the odometer had stopped around 200,000 miles. To tell the truth, the car embarrassed me, and I felt we must have been very poor indeed to have to drive it. Still, my father kept it running for years after its expiration date, until few of the old parts were left except for the steering wheel he refused to let go of.

This new Cutlass probably cost more than he'd made his first year as a lawyer, and as I sat beside him, I wished that he could have been as happy driving it as I was riding in it. But somewhere I knew deep down that nothing was worth the youth he had been deprived and that this car was a gift to himself for an imminently practical life that only allowed lines and wrinkles from worry.

Then, suddenly, we were caught in traffic, sitting on an expansion bridge, watching a barge move underneath that held hundreds of old cars, crushed, stacked on top of each other, their sad grills frowning, their windshields non-existent, their broken taillights unblinking above missing bumpers.

While we sat there, my father told me a story about how once his old car had broken down somewhere on the Pennsylvania Turnpike, and he said he had finally decided to abandon it. He left it with a rag tied through the door handle and hitched a ride to the next exit. But the car refused to be abandoned and late that night, he returned to it with a sleepy tow truck operator—my father's eyes frantically scanning the road until the shape of the old car emerged.

The road opened up wide as we came out of a crooked tunnel and white lines pointed toward a sun so large and orange that we both could do little than stare at it. Our trip to the sun coincided with my thinking about the way things might be someday—the space race, moon landings, flying cars. What was to become of us?

We pulled to the side of the road beside a field so filled with flowers I could see nothing else. Father reached behind the front seat and pulled out the longest butterfly net I had ever seen, and told me he had secretly been working on it, letting it take shape a piece at a time: the pole, long, thin and newly varnished—one that he had used to clean our gutters and knock clumps of wet leaves to the ground; the wire fashioned together and spray-painted red as smooth and sleek as his new car; and the net he made out of one of my mother's maternity dresses.

He presented the butterfly net to me, smiled, and pointed to the field; and, together we ran through flowers as if dodging raindrops, the net a long maternal funnel in full bloom. I caught everything the air offered.

The field opened up into a wide expanse where an old cabin sat. Beside the cabin, a set of rusted railroad tracks were covered in parts with dirt. Between the rails were the wooden ties, peeking up in spots like broken teeth. Coal chips of various sizes had fallen off old railroad cars and lay dirty-black in the dirt. The rails, rusty, lined up in parallel rows on their way out toward the horizon, and I imagined that if I followed them, my width, like the rails would become narrower and narrower until I became a thin horizontal line—a stick boy walking through the dust.

Father told me the cabin's history.

His father had built it.

While my father was in law school, he said, my grandfather accidentally knocked down a beehive and had raced through these fields, swallowing the bees until one of them eventually stung his heart, and he fell to the ground. During the winter, he said, the snow failed to stick to the patch of earth where his father fell.

"In these fields," my father pointed, "is a place where snow comes to die."

We sat together on the steps of the porch.

I think my father realized he had frightened me and told me my favorite story about my grandfather, who had been hired as a railroad cop during the Depression and worked the nightshift, his flashlight bobbing through the darkness as he wandered between the rails. He had been hired to prevent other men from leaving a place that no longer sustained them and had felt forever guilty about it.

Growing up in the shack beside the railroad tracks, my father said how as a young boy he always had an urge to move. Night after night, he and his father played a game: my father hiding away in some boxcar bound for leaving; my grandfather searching with his flashlight, never failing to find his son's huddled figure tucked away in one of the cars; together, they would walk home on the rails.

"I don't want to upset you, Jayson," my father said. "I want to tell you the truth."

It was at this point that the sun began to fade—streaks of purple mixed with orange and gray. I opened my eyes and half-expected the sun to have set or the sea of flowered heads to be asleep. And as we sat there, my father became even older.

"Son, if you were littler I could make up a story so you'd understand why I brought you here, why I made you the butterfly net... I don't want to talk down to you, but I think right now I need you to listen and to understand. I'm sorry, son, but Kenny Bloom died last week. He was killed in action.

I burst through the curtain of new flowers, which admitted me and then drew to a close behind me. The important thing was to keep moving, to keep the net afloat high above my head, to catch the wind, to get away, far away from this place, until I tripped over a dry patch, my mouth swallowing dirt, my mother's maternity dress deflating, falling from the sky.

My father found me and picked me up and carried me and the net to the Cutlass and deposited me inside — I waited for the car's gauges and dials to light up, for the engine to roar to life.

The title of this story was taken from the novel, The Man Who Was There, by Wright Morris.

THE PLEASURES OF SUDDEN WONDER

Before she left us, my friend Erika Cardturner and I would swing around the big light pole, Dizzy Gillespie, that held the outer reaches of our lawn; we would run round and round 'til we got dizzy. We'd laugh and stare up at the big tree, Al Kaline; we'd laugh and gaze at the weekend sky. We'd laugh and prepare for Date Nite—a weird 60s concept embraced by our collective parents; Date Nite we tried to hate, but, in the end, couldn't. Besides there was the beautiful Janice Pastiche, our kidsitter, who we loved. There was just us, acting all grown up in Erika's house in the Netherlands, imagining what we could be and what we could have been.

As easy as one, two, three, we both wondered on those Saturday couples' Date Nites what our parents talked about, where they went, what they ordered, if they mentioned us—if they even gave us the second thoughts we gave them. We doubted it very much.

Erika and I never talked about it, but we wanted to. Underneath, we were both very sad and alone. Yet, through Janice, our kidsitter, we both learned that essentially everyone *is* alone and even when my parents were out having dinner with the Cardturners—they were alone, too.

Let me step back. I fear I have gotten ahead of myself. My parents and the Cardturners predictably found themselves together because Erika and I were the same age, but after 4th grade Erika didn't go to school —although she did complete her 5th grade homework, which I collected on weekends and brought to school each Monday. Erika's house was located in The Netherlands: a dark section of the Winsome Street filled with constant shade.

On my way to and from school, I would race through The Netherlands and hear the houses answering me as I would call out their names: Ms. Books? Mr. Honesty? Mr. Sadness? This was always impossibly early in the morning or in the afternoon, and the voices of the houses would rudely interrupt the songs I was composing in my head and singing. Ms. Books would say, *"The Poetics of Space"*; Mr. Honesty would say, "Have you finished your homework, Jayson?"; Mr. Sadness would say, "Stay awhile and let's chat. Please don't leave me alone and sad."

Erika's house was large, with lots of siding, and indeed looked very alone and sad—cramped in its lot, filled up by shadows and towering trees. Not a speck of sun found its way inside. This, I believed, was the reason Erika's skin was so white and filled with thousands of very brown moles.

None of the other kids in the neighborhood would play with her. They were terrified that if she touched them they would turn into a moley mess. Surprisingly, the Winsome neighborhood kids never teased her—even they realized the limits of cruelty. Instead of mean jokes, there was silence.

I rather think Erika would have welcomed the teasing. (At least she would have felt herself recognized.) Instead, she became a mirror image of her spotted siding, hidden from all. Erika wore long sleeves all summer and winter, fall and spring.

On Date Nites, Erika would rearrange her closet—taking out and carefully examining each long-sleeved shirt—laying them all on her bed in careful stacks, still on their hangers. This arrangement and rearrangement would take hours, and she would revise, rearrange, and revise again. I watched Erika carefully place each shirt back one-by-one in her closet, as if she would have all the time in the world to wear each thing.

Date Nite came around each month, and Erika would find herself doing the very same thing once again—taking out the shirts, ordering, reordering, revisiting and revising, rethinking. As if all of this covering up really mattered or would change Erika's friendship-status quotient.

Janice Pastiche, our kidsitter, was like Dante's Beatrice. (She treated me far better than Beatrice treated her adoring Pilgrim—with only mocking concern.) Janice was a beautiful narrative: blue jeans with framed knees, a long braid of hair casually tossed to one side, a peasant blouse with a strand of wooden beads around her neck, and always with a book in hand.

She was studying something called Library Science at the University, but inexplicably she came home most weekends—I rather hoped because of Date Nite—to lounge around her parents' pool on an inflatable raft, sunglasses on, forever reading.

Janice's mother told my mother during one of those animated talks they used to have on the phone that she was worried about Janice because the girl would spend all day in bed reading. "Continually reading. Reading, reading,"--that's what I heard Janice's mother say on repeat. "One can't read all day; one eventually has to get up and do something, right?" But Janice could stay in bed all day, and the way that she would tear through books was the stuff of legend.

Although she wore rather gawky glasses, her beauty was truly beyond compare—and, when she kidsat, she didn't bother to monitor us; Janice didn't do much more than read.

Erika, who kept all of her jewelry in small boxes, carefully aligned on her dresser, couldn't, at first, really understand Janice. For Erika, watching Janice read was less interesting than watching hair dry. Of course, I felt differently.

"*You* would," Erika said snidely.

"I would what?"

"You *would* find watching her read interesting."

I wanted to say back, "Perhaps I would," but I didn't possess the sufficient confidence for such a comeback. Besides, I was both tongue-tied and outnumbered.

"*You would* because you actually look forward to Date Nites. And, I think you would be content watching her read—that would be enough for you, but not me because I'm a do-do-doer. You fancy thought as action, but I like the real thing. I like adventure. Some Date Nite, I'm going to fly this coop. You'll see."

Janice read, and I imagined the adventures happening behind her eyes. Erika watched Janice read, and I imagined all of the adventures Erika was having in her mind.

"*You* could venture out into the Netherlands with me and actually live life, Jayson. You *could* actually have a real adventure; although I'm not for certain you'd know what to do with one even if you tripped over it."

"What kind of adventure?"

"Jayson Why, I'm convinced that life is for the living, and I'm going to start living it. Not like my grandfather, who just sits in that ole' veteran's home waiting to die. God is the imagination, and the imagination is within us."

"The imagination is within us," I repeated.

"By the way, here's my homework for Monday."

Janice treated her books—mostly cheap paperbacks—like talisman. She carefully handled each, never-ever writing in them or creasing or folding their pages. Every month, she brought a new one to Date Nite, and she always left the book that she brought whether she completed it or not. Erika and I were confounded by most of them.

One night, Janice left *The Poetics of Space* by Gaston Bachelard on the side table. Neither Erika nor I wanted, at first, to pick it up. I'm not sure why the book frightened us. This one was a capital T-theory book, and Janice told us that she was reading it for an Independent Study course. She told us the book was often read in Philosophy courses and said that fast reading mitigated against Bachelard's basic precept: that a book should be read three times. First to understand its general mysteries; second to figure out the questions the author was asking; and, third to see if the author had answered them.

I could not imagine reading a book three times, but I more than suspect that Erika could. She told Janice that her father used to read hard books to her so that she could fall asleep. "Once in 3rd grade," Erika said, "Ms. G was reading an illustrated story about a talking goose. I raised my hand and said, 'Any fool knows animals can't talk.' Ms. G recoiled. 'Let's be logical about all this, Ms. G. If you insist on reading a book about animals talking, please consider *A Mid-Summer Night's Dream* because, well, at least those animals have something to say.' By the way, Jason, here's my homework for Monday."

This comment got Erika a trip to the principal for mouthing off.

The Poetics of Space sat untouched on Erika's living

room table for three off-weeks. We waited patiently for Date Nite and the return of our kidsitter with her maturity and cool clothes and cool demeanor. When Janice did appear, Erika put away her clothes, marched downstairs and told us she was reifying the term "Date Nite" into "College Nite."

College Nite it was, with Janice reading to us from *The Poetics of Space.*

Our kidsitter told us that she believed there were few limits to what kids could learn. Yes, there had been studies like the famous one about displacement where kids couldn't comprehend how a quarter could displace the level of water in a tube. Janice said that she planned to refute the displacement theory through language.

She took up *The Poetics of Space* as if she had never left it in Erika's living room. She gathered us around her and began reading aloud, "Uncovering the material" that she and her professor had uncovered earlier in the week. That way, she said, we would have a true college experience.

I don't know if you've ever had someone truly read to you, but if you have, the process changes you—it makes you more patient, more able to take on the day, more able to deal with problems as they present themselves. Janice read and strange colors—keytones: reds, yellows, blues, violets emanated and swirled up around her. She read about early houses that capture the first memories of childhood.

Erika and I scrunched up next to her on the couch cushions.

The Poetics of Space is really about the imagination more than anything else. As an extended metaphor, it suggests one should carefully examine one's first house —each of its rooms—each of the items in its particular spaces. Bachelard talks about the importance of revisiting those spaces, the basement, the attic.

"When I was growing up, we lived in a trailer," Janice said. "I wonder what Bachelard would have to say about that?" Erika and I wide-eyed each other.

"Why doesn't he just say what he means?" Erika said and scrunched up her brows. "I don't know why he has to make everything sound so complicated." She looked at me.

"*I* don't make things sound complicated," I said as if it were an accusation. "*You* don't try to but *you do*," Erika said.

"I think maybe you'd be the perfect theorist, Erika" I said.

"I don't want to be the perfect theorist. I don't want to be any theorist at all. I'm not built that way."

Janice smiled and said, "What you two are doing is called a dialectic."

"I'd call it an argument," I said.

"I'd call it stupid," Erika said.

"Shall I read on?" Janice said.

"Yes, please!" both Erika and I said.

"You know," Janice said. "Bachelard always puts me in the mind of Buckminster Fuller's geodesic domed home. I don't know why," Janice said in an off-handed way and kept on reading.

We learned about how the imagination can be more truthful than fact. We learned about how we should examine things in miniature.

"When Bachelard talks about miniature houses," Janice said, "I thought he'd discuss doll's houses. That would have been the logical leap, don't you think?"

"Yes," Erika said. "Oh yes and clothes closets."

I wasn't sure what I thought. I'd never played with doll's houses.

"You know these reading hours we spend in the Netherlands are small, but they seem so big," Janice said. "I mean take this house—your house Erika. There's so much space, and so much stuff—arguably more stuff that anyone needs. Your house is big and swelling all around us, yet here we sit, close and comfy reading and talking together in the living room. I suppose a house is as big or as small as one wants to make it."

I hadn't lived in a trailer like Janice, but one would have called my house modest. When I walked to school through The Netherlands and spied those big houses: Mr. Sadness said, "Don't be jealous, Jayson. Jealousy will make you sad." Ms. Books said, "I understand sorrow, Jayson. It's like the encyclopedia. You can read it again and again and it never changes. But please understand that although the book doesn't change, you do." Mr. Honesty said, "There's lots they don't tell you in books, Jayson. Be sure to listen to your surroundings —and to the voices that transport you."

I must admit that I *was* jealous and sad and at my

wits end. I wondered what it must take to live in such a house as Erika's. Whatever it was, Erika certainly had it. Even my parents said so: "Now *that* girl is destined for great things." My parents never said that about me–great things I suspected were far out of reach.

Janice read on about the architecture of imagination.

"I think I want to be a botanist," Erika said. "That or work in a funeral parlor."

Erika Cardturner loved flowers. She used to stand in front of flower arrangements at the grocery store, sometimes rearranging them. She'd scour through the obituaries in the newspapers and had all of the addresses to the funeral parlors within biking distance memorized.

"No one pays attention to kids at funeral parlors or cares why they are there. No one will even ask, Jayson. I promise we won't get in trouble."

"Are you absolutely 100% positively sure?" I said.

"I've always wondered why you're so worried about getting in trouble, Jayson. It's really pathological if you ask me."

"Path-o-logically," I said.

"I never worry if anyone will like me," Erika said.

Erika used flowers in the most imaginative ways. While other girls adorned their hair, she stuck them like straws in milkshakes or placed them atop grilled cheese sandwiches; she pressed their colors into the pages of her homework; she gave flowers to everyone–whether they wanted them or not.

I was terrified of flowers. I didn't like how they

smelled. I was afraid to touch them, and, sadly, looking at them didn't make me feel anything but a fear of sneezing.

"You're a humbug, Jayson. Who doesn't like flowers?"

When Janice was done reading for the evening and had left, Erika used a white rose to bookmark *The Poetics of Space*.

"White is for innocence, everyone knows that, Jayson. I believe when we finish this book, that rose will turn black. That's my theory anyway."

"Are you saying that by reading that book, we will lose our innocence?"

"You're assuming *you* are innocent to begin with," Erika laughed.

"Ah, Erika, you don't know what you're talking about," I said.

"Bookmark my words," she smiled. "By the way, here's my homework for Monday."

When Janice came to the next College Nite, *The Poetics of Space* was on the table with a white rose marking the spot we'd left off.

"Nice touch, Erika," Janice said and picked up the book.

"It's nearly perfect," Erika said.

That night, Janice read all about the importance of noticing. I noticed four smoke pipes that were perfectly aligned on an end table, stems-up in their wooden pipe holder box. One was of an old man sporting a beard. His indented eyes looked accusingly at me.

"I've noticed the wooden pipes," I said as if conjuring my words from nowhere. "How each one fits exactly into the wooden box. The old man, his beard, his eyes."

"It's working," Janice said and continued reading.

Bachelard supplemented his book with richly textured poems by other authors. Erika's eyes always widened as Janice read them. Even I was beginning to understand. Erika's house didn't feel so out-of-reach. The Netherlands didn't feel so otherworldly. Theory still didn't make sense, but parts of it kind of locked into place.

Janice continued to read about the intimacy of first houses and how the world within them might be forever mined for ideas.

"I wonder if we can imagine those early houses in the midst of living *in* them?" Janice asked.

"That's an interesting theory," Erika said. "By the way, Jayson, no homework for Monday."

I thought about my garage with the two-step walk-up, the Coke bottles that lined the shelves in rows like soldiers, our living room with its television, always on, the kitchen shelf—the counter that I pretended to parachute off of as I jumped to the carpet.

I looked around Erika's living room. The large fireplace, the bookshelves against brick walls, the big chandelier that lit up the night, the wide couch, the smoke pipes, the old man staring at me. I wondered: Is that what we do with our houses? Present them to others, as if they are the best sides of ourselves?

Late one Saturday night it all changed. Suddenly, my parents canceled Date Nites with no explanation. I wasn't very good at using the phone, but I can't believe I didn't call Erika.

Before I started noticing, I'd assumed that everything worked out. That we would see Janice again.

I did learn something from Lindle Enders.

Lindle was an odd kid, who liked to spend his free time making up stories. He lived directly across the street from Erika. On the other side of the street—not exactly in The Netherlands, but close. He noticed everything.

I went to Lindle's house the Sunday after Date Nites were cancelled. He ushered me into his father's den and with panic-stricken eyes, said that he'd heard the Cardturners and my parents fighting outside.

Lindle pointed to his father's Underwood typewriter. He picked up a single sheet of paper from his father's desk, rolled it into the typewriter, sat down, and began typing.

"What are you doing, Lindle?"

"It's too upsetting, Jayson."

"What's too upsetting?"

I stood there, not really wanting to sit down. I considered leaving but that would have been very rude. I stood there in the center of the den and as Lindle typed: I began noticing.

The large desk in the corner, covered with mounds of paper, the bookshelves that were filled with Reader's Digest Condensed Books, the metal clacker (five steel balls that played like a metronome), the bottles of unopened alcohol–mostly French champagne still in white horizontal boxes with red scripted letters. I walked over to the clacker and started it in motion. Its clacking resonated with Lindle's typing.

The big bay window in front, the steel shelving with boxes upon boxes of tissues, the old trophies that lined the top of the bookshelf, a wooden tennis racket in a wooden press in the corner of the room. I heard the cars rumbling up and down Winsome Street. I parted the curtains, and there, right in front of me was Erika's house.

"I can hear everything from here," Lindle said. "And, I like to stay up late, typing. I want to be a writer. My fingers have gotten really strong from all the typing I do. Beware when you shake my hands. I'll prove it to you. We can thumb wrestle after I compose this."

If this was so serious, why was Lindle joking?

I noticed the wooden floor, tight wooden planks that didn't look much for wear.

"I always take my shoes off in here. If you want to walk around, you should, too."

There was a green chair in the corner that seemed to want me to fall into it. The fabric was scratchy, uncomfortable, for show.

Lindle sat at his father's desk, typing.

The clacking just wouldn't stop.

Lindle's slow hunt and peck method was exasperating.

"So, I usually don't pay that much attention to what

is happening across the street. It's like the people over there live in a whole 'nother world if you know what I mean. I have curtains here, and I just don't look out the window very often. I mean the big ole' world is happening right outside, and I'm missing most of it. Both my mother and my father tell me that I am missing the world around me because I spend far too much time in my head. You ever feel like that?" Lindle said.

He paused and looked down at his typewriter.

"I know Erika did. She told me so. . . I spend a lot of time in this room, Jayson, writing. And, in doing so, I get used to the ebb and flow of the sounds at night. And there are definitive night sounds. Sounds that go with the seasons. For instance, in early winter, the sounds on Winsome Street are more pronounced. In summer, a heaviness settles over the den. In fall, the moisture in the air is heavy and feels like everything is pushing down on everything. In spring, there's a weight, you know, and the sounds of the voices in the street, unlike summer, are muffled, harder to hear. And, I tell you this because, the most important thing for a writer is the ears. Some might say the most important thing is the eyes, but this is not true. Think about it. When we write, we are listening. I read about it and they call it sub-vocalizing. You hear the voices when you write—and sometimes I get fooled into believing what I am hearing in my head is real."

Again Lindle paused, looked up at me, waited.

"I wasn't sure if the voices I was hearing outside

were real, or if I was imagining them. I didn't know for sure. I used to look across the street at Erika's house when I knew that you were there, and I'd wonder what you were both doing. Whenever the front window was open, I'd hear your voices. Well mostly your babysitter's voice. Don't you just despise that word 'babysitter'? We're nearly 12 years old."

"We called it Date Nite then College Night," I said.

Lindle looked at me quizzically.

"My parents don't really care where I go. They never worry about me because they know just where to find me. Here in this den with my own thoughts. And you know nobody really cares about characters unless we get to know them. Like what about me? Nobody really wants to get to know me. In fact, you're the first friend that I've ever invited over. I debated, Jayson, if I wanted you to see where I write. I was worried that maybe by letting someone see it would spoil this room."

Lindle looked around the room as if it was his first time seeing it.

"It's difficult to write argument scenes, Jayson. It really is—at least for me. Fight scenes are even harder. There's an internal logic that's supposed to make sense. Anyway, that's when I heard it, and I can't believe you didn't. Last night after they got home, the Cardturners and your parents were arguing really loudly. I leaned against the window to get a better look. There was Erika's father belly-to-belly with your father. Your mother and Mrs. Cardturner were just standing there in the middle of Winsome Street in their going-out clothes.

I'm not sure what they were fighting about, Jayson. I wish I knew what most adults fight about. They both said there would never be another Date Nite as long as they both lived. Mr. Cardturner told your father to go back to his little house. To stop coveting their friendship. To stay away from the Netherlands. To go back to where he belonged."

The clacking balls stopped. The metronome silenced.

"Jayson, this is the hard part. After you and your parents left, Erika's voice came out of nowhere. She told her parents to stop making other people feel small. She kept saying the word miniature over and over and over. I told you I'm not very good at describing fight scenes. Mr. Cardturner said he was sick of Winsome Street and all of it. Mrs. Cardturner said she'd had enough of the neighborhood and the trees and the lack of sun. Erika said she wanted to start anew like a fresh flower. Erika read aloud a page from a book, 'Memories of the outside world will never have the same tonality as those of home and, by recalling these memories, we add to our store of dreams. . .'"

Lindle pulled the sheet of paper out of the Underwood and handed it to me.

Dear Jayson,
Erika said she was leaving. She said she was going to a place where no one would find her. She said that she was going to shrink down and become a detail that no one would have to worry about again.

She yelled that she was tired of the arguing, tired of the anger, tired of trying to be perfect. She said she had theories that she could never prove nor articulate. She said she didn't feel very good. She said her heart was broken and she couldn't believe what her parents had done.

Your Friend,
Lindle Enders

After I left Lindle's house, I looked for Erika everywhere: in the attic, in the basement, in the garage. Once I thought I saw her shape in the siding as I walked by her house in the Netherlands. I called out to Mr. Honesty and he said, "Erika told you she was leaving. Why didn't you pay attention? This should come as no surprise, Jayson. No surprise at all, not really." I called out to Ms. Books, "Have you checked the flower arrangements at the grocery store, Jayson? Have you visited the funeral parlors?" Finally, I called out to Mr. Sadness, "Erika was very ill, Jayson. I'm surprised you didn't notice. Well, maybe you did notice. But you didn't really listen. She didn't go to school? Did you ask her about her skin? Did you notice that as Janice read each College Nite, the white rose was beginning to fade, to wither, to turn dark brown? Jayson, as you make your way through this world, promise me, please promise me as you pass by an uncertain future that you really pay attention and listen. Promise me. Please."

A month later, as I passed the Netherlands on the way to school, I paused in front of Erika's house. There was a FOR SALE sign in the front lawn. I walked up to the large red front door and rang the bell. I looked up at Erika's bedroom window, hoping for a rustle of curtains–hoping for some sign of her.

Later, I received *The Poetics of Space* in the mail—the book we'd read with Janice. Bookmarked was a passage: "To go upstairs in the word house is to withdraw step by step; while to go down to the cellar is to dream, it is losing oneself in the distant corridors of an obscure etymology, looking for treasures that cannot be found in words." The passage was bookmarked with a white rose spray painted black.

NOTES

1. A MAN'S REACH SHOULD EXCEED HIS GRASP

1. Robert Browning, "Andrea del Sarto," *Men and Women* (1855)

ACKNOWLEDGMENTS

The Book of Why has been a long, long time in the making. Many of these stories have waited patiently, have followed me and refused to let go of my imagination until they took the shape of a question mark, constantly asking why.

I'd like to thank my phenomenal publisher John Jarrett for always being patient, kind, caring and creative, allowing for the many questions involved in any book to take shape.

From the amazing cover to the interior illustrations, I want to thank L.K. Sukany. Your vision helped me to see all the possibilities in this book, and your creative vision brought Jayson Why, with hands uplifted in a Y, to life.

I'd like to thank the many authors who have supported me: Frank Thurmond, Trent Lee Stewart, Ryan Scribner, Keith Polette, Robert Olin Butler, Kevin Brockmeier, Ty Jaeger, and Peter Orner.

I'd like to thank my steadfast friend Jeff Sewald, a constant star, who is always present with his honesty, his creativity, and his questions.

I'd like to thank my amazing wife, the wonderful and wise Mary Ellen Kubit, for all of her story editing advice and for believing in the story "A Man's Reach Should Exceed His Grasp," which became the foundation for this book. Your belief keeps me going.

Thank you to my sister Lynn Ann Minnick, who literally lived some of these stories with me.

Thank you to the literary journals *Cleaver, Literally Stories,* and *East of the Web,* who published some of these stories in different forms.

Thank you to the members of the UALR English Department.

Thank you to Michael DeAnglis, Sam Gregory, John Dunn, Daniel Reimer, Belinda Blevins- Knabe, and Erick Weed for reading and believing.

Finally, thank you Mom. You are a true genius. This one is for you!

ILLUSTRATOR BIOGRAPHY

L.K. Sukany is a multimedia artist, illustrator, singer, and songwriter in the band The Damsels in Distress. Sukany earned her BFA in printmaking from Missouri State University and MA in painting from the University of Arkansas at Little Rock. She has been exhibiting art for over 25 years, and is now illustrating for publications. To date, her illustrations have also been featured in another Silent Clamor Press release *The Bankrupt Circus and Other Misadventures*.

Sukany lives with her husband and five children in a large, but snug shoe in Southern suburbia USA. You can see more of her work at paperopera.com

ABOUT THE AUTHOR

(photo credit: M.E. Kubit)

J. Bradley Minnick is a writer, public radio host and producer, and a Professor of English at the University of Arkansas at Little Rock. He has written, edited, and produced the one-minute spot "Facts About Fiction," and the award-winning program Arts & Letters Radio, a show celebrating modern humanities with a concentration on Southern cultural and intellectual work that can be streamed at artsandlettersradio.org. He is the author of *The Bankrupt Circus & Other Misadventures*, and has published fiction in *Toad Suck Review, Burning-*

word Literary Journal, Literally Stories, Inklette Magazine, Cleaver, Twelve Winters Journal, East of the Web, Litbop Art and Literature in the Groove, Rural Fiction Magazine, Café Lit, Potato Soup Journal's 'Best of 2022' anthology, and *Southwest Review.* He spends his time with his amazing wife in Little Rock, Southwest Virginia and Pittsburgh.

ALSO BY J. BRADLEY MINNICK

The Bankrupt Circus & Other Misadventures

At Silent Clamor Press, we seek to illuminate the human experience with excitement, elegance, and unflinching honesty. If this work has resonated with you — offering a profound journey or a new way of seeing the world — consider sharing your reflections with others. Your voice enriches the ongoing conversation that keeps literature vital and transformative.

www.ingramcontent.com/pod-product-compliance
Lightning Source LLC
Chambersburg PA
CBHW040514220526
45357CB00052B/1182